"I want to know why some hungry fisherman hasn't snatched you up,"

Hayden said. "It's not every woman who can cook *and* fish. And you're so beautiful...."

Tess waved away that foolishness. "Being snatched...no way. I've got a career ladder to climb. I don't have time for marriage—even for romance. What's your other question?"

"Actually, you just answered it," Hayden muttered, clearly disgruntled.

Baffled, Tess tipped her head back to look up at him. "I did?"

"You did."

"But what was it?" she persisted.

"I was just going to ask if I could kiss you... okay?" The last word was almost a growl....

Dear Reader,

The holiday season is upon us and what better present to give or receive than a Silhouette Romance novel. And what a wonderful lineup we have in store for you!

Each month in 1992, we're proud to present our WRITTEN IN THE STARS series, which focuses on the hero and his astrological sign. Our December title draws the series to its heavenly conclusion when sexy Sagittarius Bruce Venables meets the woman destined to be his love in Lucy Gordon's *Heaven and Earth*.

This month also continues Stella Bagwell's HEARTLAND HOLIDAYS trilogy. Christmas bells turn to wedding bells for another Gallagher sibling. Join Nicholas and Allison as they find good reason to seek out the mistletoe.

To round out the month we have enchanting, heartwarming love stories from Carla Cassidy, Linda Varner and Moyra Tarling. And, as an extra special treat, we have a tale of passion from Helen R. Myers, with a dark, mysterious hero who will definitely take your breath away.

In the months to come, watch for Silhouette Romance stories by many more of your favorite authors, including Diana Palmer, Annette Broadrick, Elizabeth August and Marie Ferrarella.

The authors and editors at Silhouette Romance love to hear from our readers, and we'd love to hear from *you!*

Happy reading from all of us at Silhouette!

Anne Canadeo
Senior Editor

A GOOD CATCH

Linda Varner

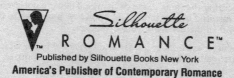

Silhouette
ROMANCE™

Published by Silhouette Books New York

America's Publisher of Contemporary Romance

Dedicated to the following
writers of romance—past and present—
who time and again inspire me to try harder:
Charlotte Brontë
Daphne Du Maurier
Mary Stewart
Victoria Holt
Madeleine Brent
Lass Small
Rita Rainville

SILHOUETTE BOOKS
300 E. 42nd St., New York, N.Y. 10017

A GOOD CATCH

Copyright © 1992 by Linda Varner Palmer

All rights reserved. Except for use in any review, the reproduction or utilization of this work in whole or in part in any form by any electronic, mechanical or other means, now known or hereafter invented, including xerography, photocopying and recording, or in any information storage or retrieval system, is forbidden without the permission of the publisher, Silhouette Books, 300 E. 42nd St., New York, N.Y. 10017

ISBN: 0-373-08906-6

First Silhouette Books printing December 1992

All the characters in this book have no existence outside the imagination of the author and have no relation whatsoever to anyone bearing the same name or names. They are not even distantly inspired by any individual known or unknown to the author, and all incidents are pure invention.

®: Trademark used under license and registered in the United States Patent and Trademark Office and in other countries.

Printed in the U.S.A.

LINDA VARNER

has always had a vivid imagination. For that reason, while most people counted sheep to get to sleep, she made up romances. The search for a happy ending sometimes took more than one night, and when one story grew to mammoth proportions, Linda decided to write it down. The result was her first romance novel.

Happily married to her junior high school sweetheart, the mother of two and a full-time secretary, Linda still finds that the best time to plot her latest project is late at night when the house is quiet and she can create without interruption. Linda lives in Arkansas, where she was raised, and believes the support of her family, friends and writers' group made her dream to be published come true.

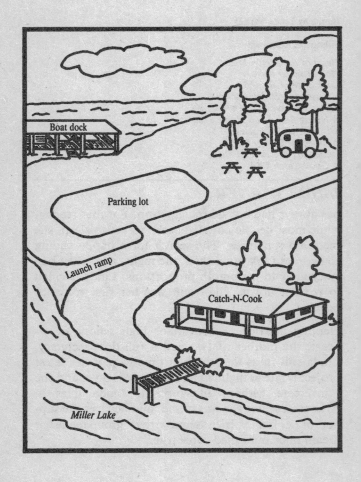

Prologue

"Grab a notepad and pencil and get right over to 8453 Penny Road. All hell's about to break loose and I want *you* to be there."

Tess Fremont, part-time society reporter for the *Jenner Springs Journal,* naturally glanced back at the desks usually occupied by the *Journal*'s two full-time reporters. Only when she found herself alone in the room did she remember that her co-workers were both out on assignment today.

Tess's heart slammed into her rib cage. She whirled back around.

"Are you talking to me?" she blurted in disbelief, suddenly wishing she hadn't embellished her experience when she applied for this job three weeks ago. Tess never dreamed she'd get an assignment so soon.

"Of course I'm talking to you," J. Q. Southerland, her editor, barked.

Tess gulped and snatched up a notepad, then stood, frantically scanning her desk for her pen. "What's at 8453 Penny Road?"

"Not a *what,* a *who.* A woman named Sharon Bogart, wife of the fishing guide at Miller Lodge. I just learned that she and Wade Waterson were seen together last night fixing a flat on his roadster."

"He's in town?" Tess asked, in her surprise not even registering the woman's name or the possible implications of "wife of" and "last night." Waterson, a hometown boy and gubernatorial hopeful in the upcoming election, usually publicized his visits to his Arkansas parents. "I didn't know."

"Neither did anyone else," J.Q. said. "Which is exactly why I suspect the very-married Mr. Waterson is here to see this Bogart woman."

Tess, now reaching for her jacket, froze. "You mean you think they're...*involved?*" Her eyes widened in shock. Wade Waterson was the epitome of the all-American male—a clean-cut, honest, family man with big plans for his home state.

"Why else would they be out on a backwoods road in the wee hours of the morning—a road that just happens to lead to his cabin by the lake?" He laughed at her expression. "Don't look so shocked. I've known that man since grade school and I'm here to tell you he's not the paragon he appears to be. Waterson has no business running for governor of this state, and an interview with his lady friend will prove it. Now hurry. A carload of night fishermen saw them and it's a cinch someone else is going to talk. This story is hot."

Hot? Try scorching... and Tess had no desire to get burned. "Are you sure I'm the right person for this interview?'' she hedged. "I mean . . . I'm pretty new at this."

"I thought you had experience as a reporter." His heavy dark brows knitted in a frown of suspicion.

"Oh, I do," she hastily replied, not adding that she'd done a grand total of two articles during the semester when she'd worked on the newspaper of the university she attended full-time. "Well . . . some."

"Then you'll do fine." J.Q. helped her into her jacket, then hustled her to the door of the office. There, Tess dug her heels into the carpet and stopped him.

"Are you sure *you* wouldn't rather go?" she asked her employer with a hopeful smile.

He shook his head. "I'm not a reporter."

Neither am I. "But what do I say to this woman? I can hardly ask if she's been sleeping with Wade Waterson."

"Why not?"

Tess gaped at him. "It's none of my business, for one thing."

"Don't be ridiculous. The public has a right to know what kind of man is running for governor of our great state. It's your duty as a reporter to give them the truth." He studied her expression, clearly baffled by her reluctance to do the interview. "Surely the daughter of Frank Fremont knows that."

J.Q. and Tess's father, a nationally known investigative reporter, went a long way back in the newspaper business. Tess had relied heavily on that old friendship when she applied for this job at the *Journal*, a ploy that seemed to have backfired.

"Face the facts. If you don't get the scoop, someone else will," J.Q. continued. Then he added, "You
need this story to put your career as a reporter on the
right track."

"Oh, yeah...my career," Tess agreed rather weakly.
At that moment, digging ditches held more appeal than
her current assignment, a sure sign she might be wise
to rethink her choice of profession. But Tess couldn't
do that—now or ever. Her reputation was at stake, not
to mention her precious father's.

"I'm counting on you, Tess. Don't let me down."

Squaring her shoulders, Tess nodded her understanding and headed outside to her car. With trembling hands, she opened the door and crawled behind
the steering wheel. A second later, she drove out of the
parking lot, headed to heaven knew what.

A resident of Jenner Spring, Tess had no problem
finding the right road and house. She pulled into the
drive and killed the engine, then glanced at her watch
and noted the time... Nine-thirty.

Stomach knotting, Tess got out of her car. She
climbed the porch steps on legs downright shaky,
pausing to catch her breath before stepping up to the
front door. Her mouth a grim line of determination,
Tess pressed her thumb to the doorbell. An eternity—
or what seemed like one—passed with no response.
Then, just as she heaved a sigh of relief, the door
opened.

Tess jumped nervously, unable to meet the steady
gaze of the man, no doubt Sharon's husband, who'd
answered her ring. Tall, lean, nice looking, he smiled

a hello that made her wish she could slink off through the grass like the snake she surely was.

"Mr. Bogart?"

"That's right."

"I'm Tess Fremont, a reporter for the *Jenner Springs Journal*. Is your wife at home?"

"Yes, but she's asleep," he replied. "She sat up all night with a sick friend."

He'd fallen for that old excuse? Tess couldn't believe it.

"May *I* help you?"

"Oh, no," Tess quickly replied. "I have to talk with her."

"What about?"

"Um, why don't I just come back later?" Tess responded, her soft heart aching for him. She had no intentions of playing tattle-tale and took a step back, only to halt when he unexpectedly stepped out from behind the screen door and grabbed her wrist.

"I have a better idea," he said in a voice so cool, Tess realized he might not have fallen for that old excuse after all. "Why don't you tell me why a reporter from the *Journal* wants to talk with my wife?"

"I-it's not important," Tess stammered. "Really."

"Tell me anyway," he responded, his voice dangerously soft, his eyes strangely mesmerizing.

Tess gulped. "I just stopped by to ask her some questions."

"What kind of questions?" he demanded, tightening his already painful grip and adding a little shake of impatience. At once Tess's sympathy shifted to his poor wife who just may have had her reasons for getting involved with another man.

"I came to ask her about Wade Waterson," she blurted in anger. "Now you let me go."

He did, but when she turned to leave, he blocked her exit. "What makes you think Sharon knows anything about him?"

Tess, already regretting her outburst, ignored his question. Rubbing her wrist, she sidestepped him and descended the three steps to the walkway.

"They were together last night, weren't they?" he asked, a question that stopped Tess in her tracks. Slowly she turned. She saw the confusion, the torture in his eyes and at once her heart went out to him again.

"Look, Mr. Bogart, I—"

A child's wail emanated from inside the house, startling Tess to silence.

The man whirled, yanked open the door and reached inside to pick up a toddler.

"Oh, God," Tess breathed, blinking against the hot tears of sympathy that sprang instantly to her eyes.

His child now in his arms, the man turned back to her. Tess blushed for her part in his tragedy.

"You'll hurt a lot of people if you print your story, Ms. Fremont," he murmured.

Tess had no reply.

"So what are you going to do?" he demanded.

She hesitated then came to a decision. "I'm going to tell my editor that your wife wasn't available. But there'll be other reporters, other newspapers."

He tensed. "There will?"

"There will." Suddenly overwhelmed with a need to make things up to him, she added, "And I'm really very sorry."

"So am I," he replied with a sad shake of his head. He looked down at his baby and sighed heavily. "So am I."

Chapter One

"**Y**o, Fishbait!" Tess Fremont called through the swing door of the spotless kitchen ruled by Rodney Spencer, owner of Catch-N-Cook restaurant on the shores of Miller Lake. Aptly nicknamed by the locals—his artificial lure collection decorated two entire walls of the dining room—Rodney could usually be found in front of his massive cookstove, frying up the catfish, hush puppies, onion rings, and French fries that made his two-year-old eatery famous.

Sure enough he was there, wearing what he always wore on Tuesdays and every other day, for that matter: overalls and a St. Louis Cardinals baseball cap. He looked over his shoulder and grinned when Tess entered the room.

"Yo, yourself. Come on in."

She did, grinning back at this distant cousin of her father. At five foot three, and one hundred and seven pounds, Fishbait probably had to run around in the sun to cast a shadow—or so her dad often teased him. "Something smells good."

"Bacon," Fishbait said, pointing toward a huge griddle on which sizzled savory slices. "Would you like some?" Before noon, customers were offered hearty breakfast fare. After that, they served themselves from a buffet.

"None for me, thanks," Tess replied, joining him. She eyed the butter-brushed slices of homemade bread, browning on the other end of the griddle, as well as the eggs, scrambled and waiting to be scooped onto a warmed plate. Her mouth watered.

Fishbait's eyes twinkled. "Sure?"

Tess nodded.

"Then how about a cup of coffee?"

"Don't mind if I do." Tess helped herself to a thick ceramic mug and a generous fill-up of the rich, black brew. She took a fortifying swallow. "Mmm. Just what I needed. I'm awfully nervous about this interview."

Fishbait said nothing for a moment, all his concentration on arranging eggs, bacon and toast on a dinner plate. Turning, he set the heaping dish on the wooden shelf under the window between the kitchen and dining room, then slapped a bell to alert the waitress. The dark-haired man next glanced at one of the several orders suspended from a wire by a clothespin, turned back to the griddle and began to pour out pancake batter.

"There's no reason to be nervous," he then commented. "You'll do fine."

"I sure hope so." Tess heaved a heartfelt sigh. "Because if I don't, J.Q. will stuff that society editor job right down my throat and make me swallow it . . . once and for all.''

"The man's a fool if he does," Fishbait commented. "Why, you've got a degree in journalism. You shouldn't be stuck behind a desk writing up weddings and obituaries. You should be out there pounding the pavement, nosing around for news, just like your dad."

"My thoughts exactly," Tess murmured somewhat glumly. "Unfortunately J.Q. doesn't agree. I thought I'd never convince him to let me write up this bass tournament. And if I don't do well on it, you can bet your favorite fishing pole I'll never get another assignment."

Fishbait flipped over the pancakes. "I can't figure out why he's so reluctant to let you report for the *Journal.*"

"Neither can I," Tess murmured, a bold-faced lie. In truth, she knew exactly why . . . and no wonder. J.Q. had reminded her at least once a day, every day, for the past three years.

Tess had long since decided the man had the memory of an elephant. And she knew deep inside that even if she won a Pulitzer Prize someday, J. Q. Southerland, owner and editor of the *Jenner Springs Journal,* would always remember her as the kid who cost his newspaper the scoop on Wade Waterson.

Fishbait dished up the golden-browned pancakes, garnished them with a curl of butter, added bacon slices and deposited the plate on the shelf. He tapped the bell, then glanced at the wall clock.

"Sure you won't eat a bite? Your interview*ee* isn't due to arrive for another fifteen minutes or so."

"I'm too jittery to eat. Who'd you get, by the way?"

"Actually, *I* didn't get anyone. When you called me, I called Carl Trent, current president of the American Bass Fisherman's Association. He didn't give me a name—just promised that one of the tournament fishermen would be here at nine o'clock to talk to you."

"Great. You're a real lifesaver, Fishbait."

"Always glad to help out."

"And speaking of helping out... The reason I came a few minutes early is so I could learn more about the ABFA."

Fishbait arched an eyebrow. "You mean you're going to interview me, too?"

"No, I'm just trying to get my facts straight so I won't ask any stupid questions. Besides—" playfully she shook a finger at him "—the competition has already interviewed you. It was a great article, too, I must admit."

Fishbait beamed. "I thought so. And I got some new customers as a result."

That didn't surprise Tess. The *Arkansas Daily,* based in the state capital, Little Rock, boasted statewide circulation—the *Journal,* only counties-wide.

Fishbait slapped more slices of bacon on the griddle. "Now what do you want to know about the ABFA?"

"Everything," Tess replied.

"Well, you've come to the right man. I'm a charter member, you know."

"Really? I *didn't* know."

Fishbait nodded proudly. "Me and some other fishermen started the group when I was twenty-three, some forty years ago. ABFA's a good organization. We promote conservation, safety and sportsmanship."

"And you sponsor tournaments that attract crowds and result in traffic jams, air pollution and litter. Tournaments that monopolize the lake and disrupt the lives of the citizens who live on it . . . at least according to the city council."

"Who are all a bunch of white-collar idiots. Bass tournaments bring in revenue—something those of us who *don't* live in lakeshore mansions need."

"Now, don't get riled," Tess scolded. "I'm here to get the other side—*your*—side of the story." She dug her brand-new notebook and pen out of her purse. "Tell me something about this weekend's tournament. I know it lasts three days and is one of several held during the year."

Her companion nodded. "The association sponsors six of them, one every month, from February through July, each in a different state. The heavyweights of those then compete in the Supertourney, held in August. This year's will be in Oklahoma."

"Heavyweights?"

"Total fish weights are tallied over the months. The twenty-five fishermen with the highest totals are called 'heavyweights.'"

"So the more ABFA tournaments you fish, the better your chances to qualify for this Supertourney."

"You've got it."

"Isn't it hard to be knowledgeable about so many lakes in so many states? I understand the tournament lake is off-limits to fishermen before a competition."

"Actually, participants are allowed to practice fish tournament waters the three days immediately preceding."

Tess frowned. "Are you telling me that the fisherman I'm going to interview this morning is here at Miller Lake to search out a honey hole?"

He smiled at her use of a term her grandfather used to describe an especially good fishing spot. "Yes."

"But that's awful. Won't he wish he was out on the water instead of in here talking to me?"

"Probably. That's why I told Carl you'd be glad to conduct your interview in a bass boat."

"You did?"

"I did."

"Oh."

"Now is there anything else you want to know?"

Still startled to learn that she would be interviewing out-of-doors, Tess had a little trouble recalling the other questions she had about the ABFA. "I...um... oh, yeah. Prizes. I want to know what sort of prizes the winners of these tournaments get."

"Boats, tackle, a car, sponsor endorsements—oh, and let's not forget the cash...$75,000 for first place in the Supertourney."

"No kidding? A man could make a living doing this, couldn't he?"

Fishbait stopped what he was doing, clearly considering her question. "Yes, but it's a tough row to hoe...especially right at first. Entry fees are steep, there's a lot of travel involved and success is not necessarily assured. I mean, some days the fish just won't bite no matter what fancy plug you toss in the water."

He cracked a couple of eggs onto the griddle, then stirred them with his spatula before continuing. "But if you stick it out, you might be the next Roland Martin, Hank Parker, Jr., or Bill Dance—winning fishermen who now host their own television how-to shows. Those guys all used to be—"

"Fishbait?"

He broke off at the sound of his waitress's voice and glanced back toward the order window, through which she peered at the two of them. "Yes?"

"There's a man out here says he's supposed to meet a reporter. Know anything about it?"

"I sure do. Show him to a table, give him a cup of coffee and tell him she'll be right out." He turned back to Tess. "Looks like you're on, kiddo."

Tess walked quickly to the window and peeked out, scanning the dining room for Fishbait's waitress. She spied her immediately, just seating a man with dark brown hair, a light blue shirt and broad, broad shoulders. Since the man sat with his back to her, Tess could see little else except deck shoes, long, denim-covered legs and a leather belt.

She did note the word *Hayden* tooled into the back of the belt, which encircled a waistline indicative of more time spent fishing than working out at a gym. Tess didn't mind the man's few extra pounds. Having once dated a football player, Tess had learned to appreciate brawn. There was nothing, but nothing, like being hugged by a male with some size to him.

Hugged? Tess almost laughed aloud at that errant thought. All she wanted was an interview with a tournament participant. Nervous as she was, it would be a miracle if she survived that.

Not for the first time Tess wondered if she'd inherited any of her famous father's talent. Reporter for one of Chicago's largest newspapers, Frank Fremont had a nose for news and the panache needed to follow through.

Tess, who'd moved to Arkansas as a teenager when her parents split, was proud of her father and wished she were just like him. That would certainly enhance her chances of surviving this probationary reporter assignment and delivering a story that would make J.Q. sit up and take notice.

On that thought, Tess squared her shoulders, walked to the swing door and slipped out into the dining room. With firm strides, she approached the fisherman's table.

"Hi, there," she said, a greeting that made him turn his head. "My name is Tess...*holy Moses.*" In a heartbeat she was hurled back in time to her first reporting assignment for the *Journal,* three years ago. She experienced again the humiliation of intruding in one man's tribulation...*this* man's tribulation.

Her spirits sank right to the bottom of that lake just outside; her confidence followed. Tess promptly forgot how to speak.

Hayden Bogart stood and took the hand she'd proffered and forgotten. He shook and released it. "So you've married. Sounds like a match made in heaven."

The words, though teasing in nature, were uttered coldly and there was no twinkle in the man's eye. Tess, who wanted nothing more than to follow her spirits and confidence out into the lake, struggled for composure.

"Actually my name is still Tess Fremont."

"And you *still* report for the *Jenner Springs Journal.*" His tone told her he rated that activity right up there with drowning puppies. "Tell me...do you get a kick out of prying into people's personal lives, exploiting their tragedies?"

Tess's jaw dropped at the unexpected insult. "For your information, I've never exploited anyone's tragedy."

"But you do pry into people's personal lives?"

Tess glared at him. "I seem to recall giving *you* a break."

He caught his breath at the gibe. "Ah, but how many other times have you been so generous?"

"None," she replied, softly adding, "I nearly lost my job over that one." The minute Tess uttered those words, she wished she hadn't. Tess wanted no sympathy from this man, and, now that she thought about it, no interview.

"Did you say you lost your job?" He sounded shocked.

Tess ignored the question. After stuffing her pad and pen into her purse, she zipped the bag shut with one agitated jerk, then raised her gaze to his.

"Goodbye, Mr. Bogart," she said, turning to stride toward the exit. Just as she reached the door, he caught up and blocked her way.

"If you lost your job, then why are you here now?"

"*Goodbye,* Mr. Bogart," Tess repeated, sidestepping him and moving out onto the porch. Quickly she descended the steps to the graveled lot.

"Call me Hayden."

Tess halted and looked back toward where he stood on the porch, his thumbs hooked through the belt loops of his faded jeans. "What did you say?"

"Call me Hayden." He actually managed a smile of sorts. "Mr. Bogart is a movie star who's been dead a very long time."

Disconcerted by his Dr. Jekyll-Mr. Hyde personality, Tess could think of no response. Whirling, she stalked over to her car parked nearby.

Hayden caught up again just as she opened the car door. "Where are you going?"

"Back to my office," Tess retorted, by now thoroughly piqued.

"But what about your interview?" Hayden questioned.

"I'll find someone else," Tess said. "It's clear that you don't want to talk. Why you ever agreed to it in the first place is beyond me." She ducked into the vehicle and settled herself behind the wheel. Reaching out, she tugged on the door to shut it, but held back as it was by Hayden, the door would not budge.

"I agreed to the interview for three reasons," he told her, crossing his arms over the top of the door and peering into the car. "One, a man to whom I owe many favors asked me to do it. Two, I need the exposure if I'm ever going to get the sponsors I need."

Tess digested his words in silence. "And the third reason?" she prompted after a moment.

"I thought I had put the past behind me. I thought I could look a reporter dead in the eye and not get sick to my stomach."

"I make you sick to your stomach?" It was Tess's turn to be shocked.

"No. But seeing you brought it all back—the pain, the humiliation, the questions. All those questions..." He closed his eyes, clearly lost in unpleasant memories, then sighed heavily and opened them again. "Look, I'm sorry I was rude to you a while ago. God knows you, of all people, don't deserve it."

Tess said nothing. Instead she unabashedly studied this man standing before her. Time had been kind to him, she decided. Very kind indeed. His face, which had filled out as much as his body, was more ruggedly handsome than she remembered. Square-jawed, with high cheekbones and eyes the color of coffee, he looked as though an ancestor might have been a member of one of the Cherokee Indian tribes that once inhabited Arkansas.

She wondered if he was still married to Sharon. If not, he was certainly married to someone, Tess decided. Though minus a wedding ring, he had that well-fed, utterly content air about him.

"So what do you say? Forgive me?"

Tess came to life. "Yes, if you'll forgive me."

He arched an eyebrow at her. "What for?"

"For coming this close—" her thumb and forefinger almost touched "—to punching you out a while ago."

Hayden looked at her with some alarm. "Think you could've done it?"

Tess nodded. "I *know* I could've. I have two brothers. But brothers or not, a good reporter never loses her cool."

"And you're a good reporter?"

"A damn good one," she said. "Unfortunately, no one knows it yet." She tipped her head back against the neck rest, once again studying him. "This fishing tournament is a hot issue in my little town, Hayden Bogart. This story would be a major boost to my career, so please be honest with me. Are you up to an interview or should I go elsewhere for it?"

"I'll give it my best shot. I swear. Pax?" He extended his right hand.

Tess hesitated, then put her hand in his. "Pax."

Though they shook on it, she felt no relief. Something told Tess this interview would be the most difficult of her career.

Most difficult of her career? She almost laughed. It would be the first and maybe the last—at least for the *Journal*—if she didn't get herself in gear.

"Are you going out on the lake today?" she asked, all business again.

"I'd planned on it." His gaze encompassed her light linen jacket, crisp white blouse, straight skirt and flats. "But if you'd rather not . . ."

"I don't mind at all," she assured him as though women wore business suits every day while fishing. Tess glanced at the sky, noting skating gray clouds that might just produce rain. Instead of worrying about that happening, she sent a thank-you heavenward. Those clouds hid the July sun, providing occasional breaks from its hot rays.

Tess toyed with the idea of making a quick trip to the Catch-N-Cook rest room to take off her panty hose, which would be miserably hot. She abandoned that idea when she saw Hayden look longingly toward the water. All Tess wanted was a story. She had no desire to ruin this man's chances to win the tournament. The panty hose could definitely be endured, just as any rain could. Her jacket, however, had to go, so she slipped out of it and left it on the car seat.

"Where's your boat?"

"That blue one over there." He pointed to a sleek fiberglass bass boat, loaded on a trailer attached to a late model pick-up truck. Blue as a robin's egg, flecked with silver, the boat gleamed as though the sun shone directly overhead instead of hiding out behind the clouds.

Tess climbed out of her car, shut the door and headed right to the vessel, parked not twenty feet away. Quickly she perused it, noting equipment that was standard to any serious fisherman: outboard motor, trolling motor, depth finder, fish locater graph, live well.

"Nice rig," she commented, turning to Hayden. Since he stood closer than anticipated, she found her eyes level with his Adam's apple. Just below that, she glimpsed a thin gold neck chain, and below that, curly dark hair, which disappeared into the neck of his cotton shirt.

Did the hair trail right down his chest and belly and disappear into the waistband of his jeans? Tess wondered. That crazy thought heated her cheeks and another, more private part of her body.

At once, Tess gave herself a mental get-yourself-together kick in the backside. A good reporter maintained objectivity at all times...especially if the re-portee was married.

"Thanks. Know anything about boats?"

"I've been fishing a time or two with my grandfather," Tess said. "Though never in anything as flashy as this."

"Think you can help me put her into the water?"

"Sure."

Hayden walked around the front of the truck to get in behind the steering wheel. While Tess watched, he expertly backed the truck, maneuvering the trailer attached to it down the concrete loading ramp into the water. In seconds, the back half of the boat was partially immersed.

Hayden put the truck in Park and set the brake, then climbed out and motioned for Tess to join him.

"I'm going to motor the boat off the trailer. When I yell, you drive the truck over there and park it. Okay?"

"Okay." Though she stepped back, their bodies brushed as Hayden slipped by her. Tess's heart turned a cartwheel—at least that's what it felt like.

Intensely aware of him, she scrambled into the truck... or tried to. Her straight skirt, which came to her knees, made that simple action rather difficult and Tess had to hoist it hip-high to step up into the vehicle.

Just as she did, she felt Hayden's gaze on her. Turning, Tess discovered that he hadn't walked on back to the boat, as she thought, but stood at the rear bumper not five feet away, watching with unabashed interest.

Again her cheeks flamed. Quickly she closed the truck door to block his view, then dropped her burning face into her hands, groaning her embarrassment.

"Tess?"

Hayden's voice, right in Tess's ear, startled her. She looked up and found him just outside the open window of the truck.

"What?" she asked, somewhat irritably.

"I've just thought of a fourth reason why I'm willing to do this interview."

That said, Hayden ambled back to the water's edge, abandoning Tess to her shattered nerves and scattered wits.

Chapter Two

"Careful now," Hayden cautioned Tess not ten minutes later as she attempted to climb aboard his boat. Again hampered by her skirt, Tess struggled and finally had to accept the helping hands Hayden offered to her. With a quick tug, he easily lifted her right up off the asphalt loading dock and onto the carpeted casting deck where he now stood.

"Thanks," Tess murmured, impressed by his considerable strength. She stepped down into the bottom of the boat, where she stashed her purse in a corner out from underfoot. After smoothing down her skirt and straightening her prim white blouse, Tess sat on the low padded seat Hayden indicated. From there, she smiled up at him, a smile that vanished when she saw what he had just retrieved from a storage compartment. "Uh-oh. I don't have one."

"That's okay," he said, handing her the life vest he held. "I brought an extra just in case. It was my wife's."

Was? That seemed to confirm that Sharon had been erased from the picture, a fact not surprising to Tess. Had someone filled her shoes? Or was this gorgeous hunk of man single again? Much too curious, Tess slipped into the vest and zipped it up.

Hayden did the same with another, larger one. "There. All set?"

"Yes."

He nodded, then settled himself behind the steering wheel in the seat adjacent to hers. With a flick of the key, Hayden started the outboard motor. Seconds later found them easing away from the loading dock and heading out across the blue-green lake.

As soon as they left all other boats and humanity safely behind, Hayden accelerated the motor to near full throttle. The nose of the bright blue vessel lifted right out of the lake as they gained speed. A rooster-tail spray of water, crystal bright in the rays of the peek-a-boo sun, shot skyward behind them and splashed silvery drops into Tess's face and arms.

She loved how the cooling breeze whipped her flaxen, chin-length hair across her face. But when a wisp of bangs blew into her eyes, Tess tipped her head back so the wind would raise them off her forehead.

Conversation was impossible above the roar of the powerful motor, so Tess didn't try to talk. Instead, she relished the moment. Her mind drifted back to the last time she went boating, four years ago. Her paternal grandfather had taken her camping on the Buffalo River to celebrate her graduation from high school.

They'd had a wonderful time, a memorable time, and Tess's only regret was that he wasn't alive when she graduated from college just last month. She knew without a doubt the two of them would have celebrated that milestone in the same way.

Tess shifted her gaze from the shoreline, nothing more than a blur of color, to the man at the wheel. She noted that he had donned a cap and turned its bill backward so the wind would not snatch it away.

Cute, Tess decided, her gaze sweeping him. Or maybe *cuddly* would be a better word. The man had a definite teddy-bear appeal that belied distinct grizzly-bear tendencies. Tess found him an enigma, an attractive, fascinating enigma, and she knew instinctively he could prove a threat to her professionalism as well as her peace of heart.

Disconcerted by that realization, she dragged her gaze back to the scenery, but her rebel thoughts stayed at the helm. Her head began to spin with questions she couldn't wait to ask. Encouraged by this burst of enthusiasm, Tess pushed aside any lingering doubts about the day and her assignment.

Everything would be fine. She would keep her cool and write the best story ever. She would prove her worth to J.Q. and to her co-workers. She would confirm—to herself as much as to everyone else—that she had what it took to succeed in the business. She would make her dad proud of her.

At that moment, Hayden slowed the boat a little and then a little more. He steered it to the left and then killed the engine, enabling them to coast on into a little cove sheltered by a wooded shoreline.

The breeze died with the motor. The air, at once humid and hot again, settled over Tess like a thick wool blanket. To get some relief from the heat, she slipped out of the padded life jacket. She then extracted her notebook and pen from her purse.

Hayden glanced down and laughed when he noticed her sitting there all primed and ready to get on with the interview.

"Looks like you're eager to get started," he commented.

"I do have a lot of questions."

"Then ask them." That said, he stepped up on the forward casting deck, where he sat on a pedestal seat and busied himself with his rod and reel. Before Tess could verbalize her first question, Hayden cast his line with an expert flick of the wrist. The second the spinner bait plopped into the lake, Hayden began to reel it in with practiced skill.

It was Tess's turn to laugh. "Looks like you're eager to get started, too."

Hayden grinned. "Yeah. This is where it's at for me."

"All you want from life?"

He shrugged. "I've got blue skies and sunshine, clear water and a fishing pole. What more could any man ask?"

Tess considered his question for a moment. "I can think of several things, actually. Companionship among them. Don't you get lonely out here all by yourself?"

Hayden reeled in his bait the rest of the way, checked it and recast before replying. "Sometimes, I guess," he admitted, his gaze never leaving the water. "But Savannah will be old enough to come out with me in another couple of years. We'll have some great times then.''

''Savannah?''

''My daughter,'' Hayden replied. ''She's four now.''

''Where is she?'' Tess asked, a question she hoped would prompt a response clarifying once and for all Hayden's marital status.

''In my camper trailer, parked about fifty yards from the boat dock.''

''*Alone?*''

''Of course not,'' he replied, most of his attention on the bait he manipulated through the water. ''My aunt lives and travels with us...has ever since Sharon and I divorced, two and a half years ago.''

''So you haven't remarried?''

''No, and that's the last question of that sort I'm going to answer. I'm here to talk about my fishing career not my personal life.'' His glittering brown eyes accused her.

''I'm sorry,'' Tess murmured, properly chastized. ''I wasn't trying to pry. I just...wondered.'' Afraid he might do a little wondering, too, namely about her burning need to find out if he were single, she quickly added, ''A reporter's prerogative, you know.''

He snorted his opinion of that.

Tess cleared her throat rather self-consciously and quickly changed the subject. ''How old were you the first time you went fishing?''

Hayden lifted his bait from the water, cast yet again, and began to crank the reel before answering. ''Two. Went with my gramps.''

"Really? My gramps took me fishing my first time, too."

"No kidding?"

"No kidding."

"Where'd you go?"

"Right here on Miller Lake," Tess replied. "Of course the area was kind of wild then. No houses to speak of."

"Did you have a good time?"

"I had a great time. My gramps was such a character and a darn good fisherman."

"What did you catch?" Hayden asked.

"The biggest ol' catfish you ever saw. Why that thing must've weighed—" Tess broke off. "Wait a minute. Who's interviewing who?"

Hayden just grinned.

Flustered, Tess glanced down at her notepad, helpfully blank, and tried to remember what she had asked Hayden.

"My first fishing trip..." he prompted softly.

"Oh, yeah," she murmured, quickly scribbling his reply. "Um...did you know right then and there you wanted to be a fisherman?"

"A fisherman? Heck, no. I wanted to be—" Abruptly, Hayden yanked hard on his rod, which bent ominously with the weight of whatever he'd hooked. With interest, Tess watched while he reeled in a fair-size bass. Mere seconds after lifting the fish from the water, Hayden worked the hook free, displayed his catch to Tess and then bent down to turn it back into the lake. "Superhero."

"Excuse me?"

"Superhero. I wanted to be a superhero."

"Oh." Somehow Tess found wits enough to record his answer. Then she frowned up at him. "You let that fish go."

"Of course. I usually do."

"But why?"

"I support the catch-and-release program."

"Catch-and-release . . . ?"

"I keep what I want to eat, and release the rest." He checked his bait and recast, then smiled at Tess. "If we don't plan for tomorrow, there'll come a day when there are no fish left in these waters. I want my daughter and my daughter's daughter to know the joys of angling."

Tess sat in silence for a moment, thinking about what he'd said. "Will all the fish caught in the tournament this weekend be released?"

"Absolutely."

"Will they live once they get back into the water? I mean, swallowing a hook must be a rather traumatic experience."

"Not if the fisherman exercises a little care. And since a dead fish cannot be weighed in, we're highly motivated to do just that. All our boats are equipped with aerated live wells, too, so the fish stays in tip-top shape until the end of the day."

"Hmm. Sounds like the ABFA is more than just a group of guys out for a good time."

"You bet we are." Hayden reeled in his line and then sent the bait flying out over the water again. "Fishermen take a bad rap. You'd be surprised what organizations such as ours do to promote fish and wildlife."

"Hmm," Tess murmured, nibbling thoughtfully on the cap of her pen. "Maybe that should be the focus of my next article."

"Good idea," Hayden said. "That kind of story would be a lot more worthwhile than ninety-nine percent of the garbage I read in the newspapers these days—"

"I beg your pardon!"

His cheeks took on a ruddy glow. "The *Journal* excluded, of course."

"Of course," she agreed somewhat dryly.

Suddenly Hayden jerked back on his rod. "Man, oh, man," he exclaimed, furiously cranking the reel. "I've got another one and it's a dandy."

Eager to see just how "dandy," Tess dropped her paper and pen and joined him on the front casting deck. On hands and knees, she peered anxiously into the churning water, gasping when she glimpsed his catch, a bass the likes of which she had never seen.

"Oh my gosh! Look at it!"

"Get the net," Hayden grunted, straining to keep the rod tip up, reel in the line and land the fish.

Tess quickly located the net, then hung over the edge of the boat while her companion manhandled his prize within reach. Sweat beaded his brow and plastered his shirt by the time Tess leaned over the side to dip the net into the water. In one quick move, she scooped up the trophy, but when she tried to bring it aboard, she overbalanced and tumbled forward.

"Whoa, now!" Hayden exclaimed, dropping to his knees to catch her by the waistband of her skirt. His rod hit the deck with a clatter that Tess didn't even hear, so absorbed was she in transferring his trophy into the boat.

"Man, oh, man," she unconsciously echoed, sitting back on her heels to examine the bass flopping on the deck. Her heart pounded with excitement, and Hayden's trembling fingers and flushed cheeks told her he must feel the same. Tess found that reaction amazing, considering the number of years he'd been fishing. Why, he must have caught hundreds, maybe thousands of fish every bit as—

"Where in the hell is your life jacket?"

Tess jumped in surprise at the unexpected question. "It's so hot that I . . ." Suddenly she guessed the reason for Hayden's shaking hands. "Oh, dear. Did I scare you?"

He said nothing, just glared at her.

"I can swim just as well as this fish, you know."

"Not if you hit your fool head on one of those submerged stumps. This lake is man-made. There are trees and no telling what else under the water."

"Oh." Her gaze locked with his. Nose to nose, neither said anything for a moment. Then Hayden shook his head and turned his attention to the fish.

Gently, he freed it from the net. Equally as gently, he extracted the bait from its mouth. Then he turned toward the side of the boat.

Tess grabbed his arm. "You're letting it go?" she demanded in horror.

Hayden heaved a sigh. "Yes. I have a freezer full of fish."

"But I don't."

"You mean you want to *eat* this baby?" Now he sounded horrified.

"If you're not going to. I love fried bass." She frowned. "What's wrong with that? You said you had a freezer full, yourself."

"I do, but..." Hayden's voice trailed to silence. "Let's make a deal. If you'll let me release this fish, you can have the next one."

"How do you know there will be a next one?"

"If there's not, I'm going to hang up my pole for good."

Silently, Tess considered his proposal. "Oh, all right," she finally replied. "But first you've got to tell me why you're so dead set on it."

"Three reasons," Hayden told her, holding up that many fingers.

"Do you have three reasons for everything?" Tess blurted before she remembered that sometimes he had *four*.

He laughed, but did not answer, instead repeating, "Three reasons. One—this fish has lived a very long time. Two—this fish has evaded many a hook and deserves its freedom. Three—I want this fish to be in this lake when I come back to this spot on Friday."

Now Tess laughed. "Okay. You win. Let it go."

Hayden did...with infinite care. That accomplished, he turned back to his companion, now standing safely in the bottom of the boat. Since she was busy straightening her skirt and blouse, he stole a moment to study her.

Though Tess's height could only be described as average, Hayden decided that adjective would not apply to anything else about her. Blond and beautiful, Tess was every man's fantasy. But *he* now held other qualities in higher esteem—qualities such as honesty, integrity and loyalty.

Of course, Hayden qualified as he watched her slip out of her flats and wiggle her stockinged toes, physical beauty did have its merits. And, he decided as his gaze slipped upward to travel the shapely length of her, he'd be less than normal if he didn't relish the view.

There was nothing wrong with looking, after all.

Look, but don't touch. Unbidden, some motherly advice popped into Hayden's head. He almost laughed aloud. He hadn't *touched*—or been touched by—anyone in a very long time, and he liked it that way. No woman, especially a reporter, was going to tempt him to risk his peace of mind...no matter how attracted he might be to her.

Attracted? The word rang in Hayden's head like a death knell. Attracted? Yes, damn it. Dangerously attracted. Why else would he have humbled himself and begged her to do this stupid interview? Lord knows he didn't owe Carl Trent *that* much.

Thoughtfully, Hayden picked up his rod and sat down again. A quick glance over his shoulder confirmed that Tess, too, was ready to get back to business.

"So where were we?" he asked, as much to get the interview on track as to get his mind off the interviewer.

"I was asking you about your childhood," she replied with a toss of her head. "Were you born in Arkansas?"

Fascinated by her hair—the color of wheat, the texture of silk—Hayden sat immobile for a moment, disrupting his usual cast, reel, cast pattern. "Was I...?

Oh, uh, no. Missouri. Is your hair naturally that color?''

"Excuse me?''

Hayden shrugged and cast his line out over the water. "Your hair is beautiful, especially when the sun shines on it.''

Tess glanced heavenward. "Which isn't very often today.''

Hayden's gaze followed hers. "No. In fact we'll probably get a shower or two before nightfall.'' He lowered his eyes to meet Tess's. "Now, about your hair...?''

"Don't you know better than to ask a woman a question like that?'' She cocked her head and gave him a pouty smile that did amazing things to his heart rate.

"Sorry,'' he mumbled, unsettled for more reasons than his faux pas. Quickly he changed the subject. "I was born in Springfield, Missouri.''

"Really? I was born in Stockholm, Sweden. That's where my mother is from—thus the hair.'' She played with a shimmery blond strand. "She was there visiting her parents. I arrived earlier than expected.''

So the color was natural. Somehow Hayden wasn't surprised.

"So you're from the Show Me State. Tell me about your folks. What do they do?''

"My dad's a retired truck driver, my mother a secretary. Since both of them were pretty busy all my life, I spent a lot of time with my grandfather. We fished every weekday and most weekends until I started to school. Then we were limited to just weekends.''

"And you never got tired of it?''

"Never did, never will.''

Tess smiled and wrote something on her notepad. "Didn't you used to guide on this lake?"

"Briefly, for Miller Lodge," he told her, unconsciously tensing at the question even though it dealt strictly with his fishing career, as requested. He reminded himself that Tess couldn't possibly know the link between that guide job and Sharon's chance meeting with Wade Waterson, a distinguished guest who just happened to be an old beau.

"So you must know the area pretty well. Do you think that will help you in this tournament?"

"I'm counting on it," Hayden commented, dragging his thoughts back to the present. He finished reeling in his line, then lay his pole in the bottom of the boat. "I'd like to try another spot or two before lunch if you don't mind."

"I don't mind." She reached for her life vest and slipped into it, a move that stretched her blouse over her full breasts. Hayden had to look away, and marveled at how she affected certain parts of his own body. Why, he actually ached for her... he, Hayden Bogart, who just last week had congratulated himself on how well he'd adjusted to celibacy after his divorce.

Now it felt as though his body had mutinied, and Hayden found his desire for Tess a nuisance, a damned distracting nuisance. Disgruntled, almost angry at this woman he barely knew and wasn't even sure he liked, he slipped into his seat and started the motor.

In seconds, they moved across the water, now mud-colored in reflection of the steadily darkening sky. Hayden steered the boat into another cove, maneuvered through the stumps dotting the water and killed the engine. He glanced at his watch and noted that it was eleven-thirty. He'd been on the lake barely two hours. It seemed like an eternity—unusual, since time always flew when he fished.

Of course, he usually fished solo. Having a woman—a beautiful woman—on board had apparently impacted on his favorite sport as much as his poor ol' libido.

"Would you mind pulling the boat a little closer to shore?" Tess's question burst into his abstraction.

"What for?"

"I have to make a pit stop," she admitted with a shrug, apparently not in the least embarrassed.

Hayden, who usually made pit stops without getting out of the boat if no one else was around, felt his face flame. "Oh, uh, sure." He stepped to the front of the boat, where the trolling motor was mounted. With the flick of a switch, he started it and, using the foot control, guided them right up to the bank.

When the boat nudged to a halt, Tess stood and shed her life vest. She stepped into her shoes, then joined him on the front casting deck. Waving aside the hand he offered, she jumped right off the boat and onto the grass.

"Darn," she murmured as her shoes sank into the water-logged earth, but she didn't stop...just headed for the cover of the thick undergrowth.

Hayden couldn't help smiling at the sight of this woman in her dress clothes, vanishing into the wilderness.

Five minutes passed, then five more. When another five ticked away, Hayden began to get concerned.

"Tess?" he called, anxiously scanning the bank. When she didn't immediately reply, he stood, fully prepared to hike inland to look for her. *"Tess!"*

"I'm right here." She stepped into view at that moment and smiled at him as she made her way back to the boat. "Sorry I took so long. I just had to get rid of these panty hose." She held up a fistful of stockings. "Hope you don't mind."

Mind? Hayden's gaze caressed her golden-tanned legs. He cleared his throat and shifted slightly to ease the sudden tightness of his jeans. "Why would I mind? You must be awfully uncomfortable in that getup."

"Actually I'm not...now, anyway." She walked to the nose of the boat and assessed it. "I think I'm going to need a hand here." In a heartbeat, Hayden moved to reach down for her. Tess gave him her free hand, hitched her skirt up a couple of inches and jumped aboard. "Thanks," she breathed before stepping down onto the deck of the vessel.

Hayden watched as she stuffed her stockings into her purse and made herself comfortable again. When she picked up her notebook and began to read what she had written, he shook himself out of his stupor long enough to start the trolling motor again and move the boat a few yards away from the bank.

"Ready for some more questions?" Tess asked.

"Ready," he replied, grateful to be getting down to business again. Between her questions and his fishing, he might be able to keep his thoughts clean.

"What are your goals, Hayden? What happens after you win the Supertourney?"

He smiled approval of her positive attitude. "If I win, I'll get a major sponsor and hopefully star in a few of their commercials. If those work out, I might be invited to host my own television show. You've seen the fishing shows on cable, haven't you?''

Tess nodded.

''Then you know the format. Think anyone would turn on their sets every Saturday morning to watch me fish for thirty minutes?''

''I know I would.''

His heart skipped a beat. He found himself enormously pleased and acknowledged that perhaps he did like Tess after all...more than he'd first thought, anyway.

''And I can think of at least three girlfriends of mine who would, too.''

Hayden arched an eyebrow in surprise. ''All these friends of yours enjoy fishing?'' Statistically more males than females enjoyed angling as a sport.

Tess laughed. ''No. All these friends enjoy man-watching. They probably wouldn't even notice you were fishing.''

Hayden's whole body flushed in response to her teasing. It had been too long since he played any man-woman games. He didn't know how to act anymore.

''Moving right along,'' he prompted, highly disconcerted, again off balance. Tess surely had a way of doing that to him.

Clearly amused by his discomfort, she got on with the interview as suggested. She questioned him with a reporter's dedication regarding tournaments—past, present and future.

He told her all about them as well as about his boat, his tackle and his technique. He described his life on the road. He even shared a few anecdotes—heretofore untold stories about some stupid mistakes, some hard-learned fishing lessons.

And all the while, he cast, reeled, cast, reeled and, if he were lucky, unhooked a large- or small-mouth bass, which he deposited in the live well for his hungry companion.

Hayden moved the boat several times during this period. At one o'clock, he moved yet again—to a shady meadow at the far side of the lake so they could picnic on the lunch he had brought.

"Hungry?" he asked when the boat nudged the gently sloping bank.

"Starved," Tess admitted.

"Then let's have some lunch. I'll be glad to share mine." He reached for the ice chest stashed to one side of the boat.

Tess shook her head. "Oh, no. I couldn't take your lunch away from you...."

Hayden said nothing; he just opened the chest and tipped it slightly to display the contents: ice and canned drinks on the bottom, sandwiches, chips, cake and fruit in the food tray. "As you can see, my aunt always packs way too much." He sighed and shook his head. "And since I hate to throw away good food, I always eat it all. You'd be doing me a big favor if you helped me out."

Tess eyed the food with obvious pleasure and licked her lips. "Well, if you put it that way..."

"I do," Hayden said with a grin. He shut the lid on the chest and got to his feet so he could pick it up. "Just follow me," he instructed as he took a giant step out of the boat and headed up the grassy slope, arms laden, to a shade tree he knew well.

Chapter Three

"This is wonderful," Tess murmured sometime later around a bite of luscious chocolate cake that could only have been made from scratch. "Be sure to give my compliments to... what is your aunt's name?"

"Gracie Morgan, and I'll certainly tell her how much you enjoyed the cake," he promised from across their table—in actuality, the top of the ice chest. Though Hayden sat right on the lush green grass, Tess used her life vest as a cushion to protect her skirt from stains.

"Did you say she has lived with you and your daughter for two years?" She took another bite of cake.

He hesitated slightly before speaking. "Two and a half, actually."

"And she and Savannah always travel with you?"

"Most always."

"Do they like the gypsy life?"

"Yes."

Tess opened her mouth to ask another question, then shut it again when she noticed his slight frown. Belatedly, she realized that Hayden's answers had grown shorter with each query, a sure sign she'd once again stumbled onto the no-man's-land of his private life.

She hadn't intended to, of course. Just naturally wanted to know more about this fisherman she already considered a friend. Obviously Hayden felt differently. She was still nothing more than a pesky reporter to him.

Tess found that actually hurt her feelings a little—a baffling response that disconcerted her almost as much as her real motives for asking these "personal" questions. A truly dedicated reporter would feel more than friendly curiosity about Hayden. A truly dedicated reporter would burn with the desire to solve the very mystery that first brought them face-to-face, three years ago.

And what a mystery it still was. In spite of the fact that a whole carload of fishermen claimed to have seen Wade Waterson and Sharon Bogart together on a back road in the wee hours of the morning three years ago, the tryst was never proved.

Neither Sharon nor Hayden talked to the press—from the Little Rock reporters, who, Tess remembered, descended on Jenner Springs in the days that followed, or the national reporters, always on the prowl for some juicy tidbit or other. Waterson, of course, loudly disclaimed everything, so the story was eventually chalked up to too many fishermen drinking too many beers.

Tess, who also knew the truth, never talked, either. The little she knew was not enough to print anyway, and she would most likely have lost her job for not getting the rest of the story. Tess couldn't take that risk. Her father would never have survived the humiliation.

And since Waterson lost the election, in the end no one was hurt...at least, that's what Tess told herself. Never mind that he'd already announced his candidacy for the next governor's race, just over a year away. Surely the man had learned a lesson from his scrape with scandal. Surely he now walked the straight and narrow....

"What made you decide to be a reporter?" Hayden asked, a question that seemed to indicate their thought processes might have been parallel.

She had to think for a moment, which surprised her. "It just seemed the natural thing to do, I guess. My dad's a reporter, too. He works in Chicago for the—"

"Tribune!" Hayden exclaimed with a snap of his fingers. "Frank Fremont. I just made the connection." He grinned. "I've read a lot of his pieces. They're very good."

"You mean you *like* him?" Tess teased, as though shocked. "A reporter?"

"Hey," he retorted. "Your dad has exposed a lot of political graft. If all reporters were as honest and gutsy, maybe our lawmakers would clean up their—" He halted abruptly, shifted his gaze from hers, then cleared his throat rather sheepishly. "Would you like an apple?"

"An...? Oh, uh, no thanks," Tess replied, biting back a smile. Apparently Hayden thought reporters were okay...when he wasn't involved in their quest for truth. "I've eaten way too much already."

There was a moment of silence, then Hayden softly asked, "Have you always wanted to follow in your dad's footsteps?"

"Not exactly," Tess admitted. "I've always loved to write, though. And since Dad thought I showed some talent, he urged me to give his profession a try." She met Hayden's searching gaze. "Majoring in journalism was a small price to pay for his footing the bill for my degree. I know it wasn't easy for him. Reporters—even good ones—aren't exactly overpaid and he has two other children by the wife he has now. He helped, though, and pulled strings to get me this job. Dad and the owner of the *Journal* used to work together. They both believe I should learn the basics here—the *Journal* may be small, but has won a lot of awards—before I move on to bigger and better things."

"I . . . see."

For some reason, those words put Tess on the defensive. "You see what?"

"The reason for your live-and-let-live attitude. It's very unusual in a reporter, you know, and probably stems from your lack of commitment to your career."

Tess caught her breath. "Lack of . . . ? For your information," she retorted, "I'm fully committed to my career. As for my *attitude,* as you call it, don't be misled. I'm not the tenderheart I was three years ago. I can be as tough as the next reporter when I need to. Luckily for you, my assignment is to report the fisherman's side of this tournament controversy and nothing more." She brushed a piece of nonexistent lint from her sadly wrinkled skirt, then raised her defiant gaze to his again.

He said nothing in response, a fact Tess found infuriating.

"I'm doing exactly what I want to do with my life, Hayden Bogart," she continued. "And someday you're going to see me on television—the next Barbara Walters."

"It'll take years to gain that kind of notoriety," he warned.

"I have the time," she advised him with a toss of her head. "And I have the drive, too, by the way. I will succeed. You'll see." Ready to change the subject, Tess reached for her soft drink. Just as she tipped her head back to take one last swallow, a drop of rain hit her square in the eye. "Uh-oh."

Hayden looked at her over his own soft drink and arched an eyebrow in silent questioning.

"I felt a drop of rain," she explained, glancing up at the threatening sky. No sporadic bursts of sunshine now, she realized with a start. Heavy black clouds had rolled in from the southwest, bringing with them a brisk, rain-scented breeze.

Hayden, his eye now on the turbulent heavens, groaned softly and leapt to his feet. "We'd better get out of here," he told her, gathering up the remains of their lunch. "I'd rather be off the lake when this storm hits."

Tess helped him clear, and in minutes they finished and made tracks to the boat. There Hayden boosted her aboard, then quickly joined her in the bottom of the boat. While Tess slipped into her life vest and her usual seat, he stashed the ice chest and donned his own vest. In moments, he settled himself behind the steering wheel and started the motor, but not before rain began to sprinkle down in earnest.

Hayden wasted no time in guiding the boat out into the middle of the lake and speeding toward the dock. Their ride, naturally a bit rough on the now-choppy water, took a full half hour. And by the time Hayden slowed the engine and closed the last yards to shore, a full-fledged storm raged, complete with special effects.

Lightning forked jaggedly across the sky; thunder rumbled, shaking the ground beneath their feet. Rain poured... onto Tess's head, into her eyes, down her neck. A little frightened to be on the water, she heaved a sigh of relief when they finally reached the loading ramp in safety.

Hayden made short work of docking the boat. He guided it to the side, out of the way of any other incoming vessels and then jumped onto the asphalt ramp to hold it steady for Tess.

Blinking against the downpour, Tess scooped up her purse and scurried to the front of the boat. There she poised on the casting deck for a second, gauging the length of her jump. Hayden reached out a hand, which she took, and wishing she wore jeans instead of her straight skirt, Tess jumped.

At that very moment, the boat dipped sharply in its own wake, now slapping the shoreline. Caught off guard, hampered by her skirt, Tess tumbled forward... right into Hayden's outstretched arms.

He caught her with a grunt of surprise. No less startled to find herself pressed so suddenly against the length of him, Tess clung for dear life. In two steps,

Hayden carried her away from the water, but instead of setting her on her feet at once, he held her, tightly, for several disconcerting seconds before lowering her, a millimeter at a time, to the ground.

Tess, with her admitted susceptibility to hugs from large men, could barely breathe by the time her shoes touched the wet asphalt. Breathless, flustered, she eased free of those powerful arms of Hayden's and took a step back. But her shell-shocked knees immediately buckled. Luckily, Hayden rescued her again—this time from a hard landing on her backside.

"You okay?" he asked, words barely discernible in the downpour.

"Yes," Tess murmured, thoroughly embarrassed, hoping he thought she'd lost her footing in a puddle. Her face flamed, and she marveled that the rain didn't sizzle when it splashed onto her burning cheeks.

Hayden murmured something she didn't understand, stared down at her for a full minute, then glanced over his shoulder toward the camping area.

"Why don't you come over to my place and dry out before you get in your car?" he suggested, his voice now raised so he could be heard over the roar of wind and rain.

Not at all eager to get the fabric seats of her brand-new vehicle wet, Tess quickly agreed. She wanted to meet Gracie and Savannah anyway.

Hayden led the way to the camper, large and ultra-modern. He knocked briskly on the door before opening it, then ushered Tess inside, where she stood dripping on the floor while he made short work of introducing her to his family.

"Savannah, Gracie, this is Tess Fremont. Please get her a towel." His daughter, red-haired with wide blue eyes and a generous sprinkling of golden-brown freckles, scrambled to do her father's bidding. She returned in seconds with a fluffy yellow bath towel.

Tess made use of it, very aware of Savannah's—and Gracie's—avid interest in the procedure. Hayden, meanwhile, disappeared into a room at the back of the camper, no doubt to change clothes.

An awkward silence followed, during which Tess's hostesses eyed her with open curiosity. Rain slashed against the metal roof; strong winds tore at the camper. Extremely uncomfortable under their scrutiny, Tess fumbled through her brain for something—anything—to say while she squeezed the last drops of moisture from her hair.

"Hayden shared his lunch with me," she finally blurted. "Your cake was wonderful. Just wonderful."

"Why, thank you," Gracie replied, clearly pleased. Her plump cheeks glowed rosy red. "An old family recipe. His favorite."

"I knew any dessert that good had to be homemade," Tess said, words that made a friend for life if the woman's bright smile was anything to judge by. At once, Tess felt more at ease.

Suddenly Savannah turned on her heel and dashed down the hall after her dad, long curls airborne. Tess, eyeing her purple-and-white polka-dot panties, which peeked from under an equally colorful sundress, had to smile. What a cutie. No wonder Hayden couldn't bear to leave her behind while he trekked the tourney trail.

"Would you like to sit down?" Gracie asked, pointing to the eating booth.

"I'd better not," Tess replied. She took note of the woman's floral duster and fuzzy blue house shoes and was reminded of her grandmother. Gracie and Tess's Granny Fremont were similarly shaped—rather round—and both had strikingly beautiful silver hair. "I'm soaked."

"You certainly are," Gracie agreed, shaking her head, clucking like a mother hen. "But you won't hurt these old benches. They're just vinyl."

Since they were, indeed, and therefore waterproof, Tess gratefully sat at the table as invited.

"Now how about a cup of coffee? You don't want to catch a chill."

"Only if you have some made." Though anything but cold, Tess needed something to do with her hands now that she had dried herself as much as she could.

"Oh, I keep a pot going all day, honey," Gracie assured her as she shuffled to get a mug from the cupboard. Tess took it from her moments later and sipped the dark brew, which tasted rather wonderful after all. When she lowered the mug again, it was to find that Savannah had returned . . . with a comb. "Oh, dear. Is that a hint?" Tess couldn't resist teasing when the child thrust it at her.

"Savannah!" It was Hayden, also just returned and looking wonderful in form-hugging sweats and a T-shirt that matched his flushed cheeks.

"She's just trying to help me out," Tess told him. She smiled at the child, who hadn't said a word since Tess walked through the door. "Do you have a mirror, too?"

Copper curls bounced the affirmative, then Savannah took Tess's hand and tugged until Tess got to her feet and followed her to what turned out to be the bathroom.

"Thanks," Tess murmured as she stepped inside. One glimpse in the big mirror over the sink confirmed her worst suspicions. Not only was her hair a mess, her waterproof mascara had melted and puddled under her eyes. She realized with dismay that she looked like someone's pet raccoon.

No wonder Gracie and Savannah had been struck speechless when she burst through their door.

Chagrined by her bedraggled state, Tess snatched a tissue out of a nearby box and rubbed off the black goo—a rather painful procedure without any cleansing cream to aid her. Then, and only then, did she notice how her white blouse, wet and virtually transparent, clung to her lace demibra.

"Oh, for—!" she exclaimed, mortified. She untucked the hem of the blouse and flapped it in an attempt to air dry the garment. Several long minutes passed and the pounding of the rain became a soft patter before Tess finally admitted defeat. With a snort of disgust, she loosely retucked the blouse and combed her hair as best she could. Then she opened the door and stepped out into the hall.

With quick steps she walked back to the kitchen, where Hayden and Gracie both sat at the table, sipping coffee. Savannah, a glass of orange juice in hand, sat in a child-size rocker nearby.

"Better?" Tess asked her.

The child nodded solemnly, but still said nothing.

"Thanks for letting me use your comb and mirror." Tess bent down to pat her shoulder, then straightened and turned to Gracie and Hayden. "And thanks to you two for the coffee and the towel. Now I hate to rush off, but it sounds like the rain has slowed down a bit—"

"You're leaving so soon?" Gracie sounded honestly surprised. "I thought you might have dinner with us. I have a stew in the slow cooker. It'll be ready in a couple of hours."

"Oh, I couldn't possibly stay that long," Tess responded, wondering at the invitation. After all, Tess was only a reporter trying to interview the woman's nephew. It wasn't as though she and Hayden were involved on more than a professional level . . . or ever would be. "I have to go home and write up my notes. And there's the little matter of these wet clothes. . . ."

"I'll bet you would like to get out of them," Gracie replied with a smile of sympathy. "We'll give you a rain check for the stew." She chuckled softly at her little joke.

"Thanks," Tess said, biting back a smile. Careful to keep her arms crossed over her chest, she moved toward the door, only to halt abruptly and turn back to Hayden. "Do you have a spare ice chest I can borrow for my fish?"

"Oh, Lord. I'd forgotten all about them." Hayden rose and walked over to a cabinet. He retrieved a small box from one of the shelves and then drew a plastic bag out of it. "This should work just as well." When Tess reached out, he shook his head. "No, ma'am. You stay here. I'll get the fish."

"Don't be silly," Tess replied. "You just dried out. I'll go."

"You'll stay." That said, he opened the door and descended the few steps. Then with long strides, he headed toward the boat dock through the sprinkling rain.

With a huff of exasperation, Tess turned to Gracie, who just chuckled again. "You'll get used to him, honey," she said, words that seemed to indicate she fully expected to see Tess again.

Tess honestly didn't think that would happen, especially since Hayden had just eliminated a perfectly good reason by putting the fish in a plastic bag instead of an ice chest she would've had to return. Suddenly a little depressed by it all, Tess decided not to hang around as ordered, but said her goodbyes and hurried after Hayden.

Just a few yards behind him, however, she slowed her pace and hung back a little, relishing the view. Hayden's soft sweats clung to his muscular hips, thighs and calves. No excess ounces there, Tess noted, nor on his upper back, shoulders and neck. Just his waistline needed trimming up...and as far as she was concerned, he needn't bother. Tess found Hayden's love handles rather endearing.

Endearing? Try sexy as hell.

Tess sighed, almost regretting that she had no excuse to see Hayden again now that she had all the information needed for her article. She'd really enjoyed their day together. Wouldn't mind going out with him in his boat again—only the next time she would be properly attired, with a rod of her own. Of course, she would have to buy herself a fishing license first, something she hadn't bothered to do since her grandfather died.

At that, Tess bit back a dry laugh and closed the remaining distance to the boat into which Hayden had now climbed. A lot of use she had for a license these days. Not only did she not have anyone with whom she could fish, she didn't have time for anything but her job.

And what a job... Full-Time with capital *F-T,* Tess thought with a rueful shake of her head. She couldn't count the Saturdays and even Sundays she'd devoted to the *Journal* in the past three years as mail clerk, telephone operator, receptionist, advertising coordinator, society editor and now reporter.

Publishing a seven-day-a-week newspaper took a lot of blood, sweat and tears. J.Q. expected his small staff to give their all. He paid them well for their time, of course, but there were days Tess wondered if she wanted to slave like this for the rest of her life. Only her belief that her broad knowledge base would help her land the job of her dreams kept her hanging on.

"How many are there?" Tess asked when she joined Hayden where he now knelt on the deck of the boat, taking fish from the live well.

Apparently unaware of her approach until then, Hayden jumped and then glared at her. "I thought I told you to stay put."

"I seldom do what I'm told," Tess sassily advised him.

Hayden digested that in silence, then heaved a sigh and turned back to his task. "There are four in here. Want me to clean them?"

"Thanks, but I can do it." Why should Hayden clean fish he wasn't going to eat? Tess reached out for the bag, now secured with a rubber band.

Instead of handing it over, Hayden set it on the casting deck, jumped out of the boat, then picked it up again. Touching his fingers to her elbow, he guided her to her car.

After taking the package from him and placing it on the floorboard of the back seat, Tess offered Hayden a smile and her hand. "Thank you for the interview. I hope it wasn't too painful."

He chuckled and took her hand. "It wasn't half bad. In fact, I'm kind of sorry we got rained out." When he released her, he frowned slightly as though he'd just thought of something. "Do you have enough information for your article? I mean...I did promise you the entire day and it's only—" he glanced at his watch "—two."

"I have enough," she replied.

"Sure? You can go out with me tomorrow, too, if you need to." He shrugged rather self-consciously. "It was kind of nice having someone around to watch me show off."

"Well...I do have a few more questions," Tess heard herself reply. Disconcerted by the lie that fell so easily off her lips, not to mention her wildly racing heart, she quickly added, "But I can only spend the morning with you. I have to do some work in my office. In addition to reporting for the *Journal,* I'm society editor."

"Oh, yeah?"

"Yeah."

"What, exactly, does that involve?"

"Writing up weddings and obituaries, for one thing. I also report the activities of the locals. Mrs. So-and-So went to Atlanta to visit her sister. Miss Whatsit hosted a shower for Miss Bride-to-Be—that sort of thing."

"Do you like it?"

"Sometimes it's fun."

"But you still think you'd rather be a reporter."

"No, I *know* I'd rather be a reporter," she amended.

He said nothing for a moment, then sighed and shook his head as though unable to comprehend how anyone could want to do something so dastardly.

"You really have a thing about them, don't you?" Tess couldn't help but comment. After all, she had been nothing but nice to him today, avoiding topics he wished to avoid. That, if anything, should have changed his opinion of reporters.

"If I do it's no wonder," he replied. "I learned the hard way just how nosy, aggressive and conniving they can be. I had a hell of a time protecting my family and Sharon's three years ago. Forgive me if I still don't trust a one of them."

"I like that!" Tess exclaimed, insulted.

"Oh, I didn't mean you," he made haste to assure her, a comment Tess wasn't certain how to take. "In fact, I consider myself pretty darn lucky that you're the one doing this interview."

"Does that mean you trust me?"

Did she imagine his hesitation? "I, uh...invited you back, didn't I? Now I'm pulling out of here at 6:30 sharp tomorrow morning. Meet me at the dock?"

"I'll be there," Tess promised, slipping behind the steering wheel of her car. "And I'll bring lunch this time."

"That isn't necessary," Hayden assured her.

"I'm still going to do it."

"All right, then. Gracie will probably appreciate the day off." He shut the door and took a step back so she could start the car.

"See you," she called through the window glass before pulling away and heading down the road to the highway.

See you, her words echoed in his head. *See you, see you, see you.*

"And why will she see me?" he muttered aloud with some sarcasm. "Because I asked her to, that's why."

Shaking his head in wonder, Hayden made his way to the camper. He didn't even notice that a new wave of rain had reached the area and now pelted down on his still-damp hair. All his thoughts were on last night. How he'd dreaded today's interview and all the questions he would have to answer...so much that he hadn't even slept well.

Yet he'd just invited Tess back to ask more—Tess a reporter "fully committed" to her career, a reporter who was no "tenderheart," who knew the truth about Sharon and Wade and just might be desperate enough to print it this time around.

Amazing. Baffling.

"Pretty damned stupid." And he couldn't imagine why he'd done such a thing.

Or couldn't he? Cursing his traitorous hormones for tricking him into spending more time with Tess, Hayden vowed that tomorrow's outing would be different. He would answer only those questions to do with his fishing and would ask none of his own. He would not get involved in Tess's life; he would not let her get involved in his. And when they parted at noon, it would be for good and forever.

That decided, Hayden yanked open the door and stalked inside. He found Savannah at the table, perched on an upturned cooking pot that served as a booster chair. Before her lay a coloring book and crayons. Gracie, looking rather tired to Hayden's critical eye, stood at the sink, rinsing out her coffee cup.

"Are you feeling all right?" he asked, taking his place at the table again. He reached out to flip on the radio sitting on the edge of the counter. Immediately, the haunting refrain of a country ballad filled the camper.

"I have one of my headaches," Gracie replied.

"Why didn't you tell me you were sick?" Hayden scolded, turning the radio back off. Gracie certainly didn't need the extra noise. "I didn't have to go out today."

"I felt fine when you left."

"Stretch out on the couch and put up your feet. Dinner's on me tonight."

Chuckling at his generous offer—the food *was* virtually prepared—Gracie sank onto the couch that converted to the bed Hayden occupied every night. Savannah always holed up in the bunk above him, while Gracie slept in the tiny compartment at the other end of the camper. If they had overnight guests—Hayden's younger brother, for instance—the eating booth was converted into a guest bed.

"Your new friend seemed very sweet," Gracie commented once she was settled under a hand-knitted afghan.

Hayden, well aware of how his busybody relative loved to make something of nothing, tensed slightly and reached for his coffee. "She's not a friend—she's a reporter."

"Whatever she is, I hope she didn't ruin her clothes. That skirt of hers was linen."

Hayden grunted in reply and sipped the lukewarm brew, hoping his lack of enthusiasm for the conversation would end it.

No such luck.

"Wasn't Miss Tess pretty, Savannah?" Gracie said next. "So tall and slender."

"She has big breasts," the child replied without taking her eyes off her work.

Hayden nearly spewed his drink. Choking, he grabbed for one of the napkins tucked into a plastic holder at one end of the little table.

"Do you think they're too big?" Gracie asked Savannah, a question that earned her a killing look from Hayden. He saw that her eyes twinkled and silently rued that Morgan sense of humor that kept things lively.

"No," Savannah said after a moment's serious consideration. She raised huge blue eyes to his. "Do you, Daddy?"

Hayden swallowed hard. "I, uh, no. No, I don't."

"She had a pink bow on her bra," Savannah then confided. She giggled behind her hand. "I could see it real plain."

Thoroughly embarrassed, vividly recalling that tantalizing pink bow on that equally tantalizing, very lacy bra, Hayden looked once again in Gracie's direction. Without words, he begged her to change the subject.

"Wasn't her hair pretty?" Gracie said, obliging him with a sweet smile.

"Yes, and that's just how I'm going to wear mine when I grow up," Savannah informed them.

"You'll have to color it," Gracie replied. "I wonder if hers was natural?" she then asked, as though Savannah were an adult instead of a precocious four-year-old. Hayden silently vowed to give his aunt a vacation as soon as possible. Obviously she needed time with her peers.

But to his amazement, Savannah gave this question serious thought, too. "I just don't know," she finally murmured, then turned again to her exasperated dad. "Do you?"

"Her hair is naturally that color," he said.

"How can you be so sure?" Gracie asked, watching him closely...too closely. Hayden felt seventeen again, and he hated it. "It's awfully hard to tell these days."

"I asked her, okay? Now can we talk about something else?"

Silence greeted his growling request. Gracie and Savannah exchanged a look, then Savannah turned back to her father, who wished he hadn't been so candid. "You're not supposed to ask things like that," she scolded, shaking her finger at him.

In spite of himself, Hayden squirmed under her censure. Irritated at the role reversal, he reached for a red crayon and began to help his daughter, a rather haphazard effort if her huff of impatience was anything to judge by.

"You're supposed to do it all in one direction," she curtly informed him. "Like this." Savannah took the crayon and demonstrated proper technique. "And you have to stay in the lines."

Abruptly Hayden tossed down the crayon, snatched up his coffee cup and dumped the less-than-tasty liquid into the sink. When he turned back around, it was to find two pairs of eyes on him—eyes full of surprise and curiosity.

"Are you mad at me?" Savannah asked.

"Of course not," he replied, embarrassed that his behavior had prompted such a question.

"At Gracie?"

"No."

"At Tess?" She pressed on with a child's persistence.

"Not at Tess, not at anyone," he murmured, a half-truth. In reality, he was pretty darned irritated with himself. "And I'm sorry if I made you think I was." He stooped to plant a kiss on the top of her precious head. "Now I'm going to load up my boat. I'll be back in a bit." That said, Hayden stepped to the door and ducked outside, smoothly dodging Gracie's knowing smile and Savannah's probing questions.

It was just too bad, he thought, that he could not escape the vivid fantasies evoked by his hell-raising hormones. Hayden knew he'd be lucky to get any sleep at all again that night. And if he did…well, his dreams would probably be haunted by a certain blond beauty with eyes as gray as storm clouds and a smile as bright as a sunny day.

Chapter Four

After loading his boat up on the trailer and driving it to the parking area adjacent to his camper, Hayden walked over to some nearby picnic tables and sat down on a rain-slicked wooden bench.

He didn't even notice the wet. He simply sat in silence, hoping a few more minutes in the great outdoors would help him put his worries in perspective. After all, a thirty-year-old fisherman with a skeleton in his closet surely didn't amount to a tadpole in the stream of life.

Why, there were probably millions of people out there with worse problems than whether or not the rain would affect this Arkansas bass fishing tournament or how big and empty Hayden Bogart's ol' bed would be now that he'd held a woman again.

Maybe even billions.

Nonetheless, Hayden heaved a doleful sigh and leaned back against the tabletop. For the first time in months, he thought about Sharon. In ways, Tess reminded him of his ex-wife. She not only had big dreams and the determination to achieve them, but by profession, was most likely a user, too.

For that reason he almost dreaded tomorrow and the hours he would spend carefully guarding his tongue, keeping his distance. How he wished he could devote his energies, instead, to developing a personal relationship—a *very* personal relationship—with Tess, the first female to pique his interest in a long, long time.

Hayden wondered why this story was so important to her. The personal questions she asked—though few—worried him. She *was* the only person besides immediate family who knew the truth about Sharon and Wade.

And no matter how pure her motives originally, this unexpected reunion with him was bound to impact. After all, she'd once nearly lost her job because of this very story. She'd be less than human if she weren't tempted to redeem herself now that Waterson was back in the news again.

As for developing a relationship with her...Hayden almost laughed at the very idea, knowing he'd do well to keep his distance and avoid emotional or physical attachment to Tess—no matter how tempting. Seeing her had not only brought the past back, but dropped it squarely between them, a barrier he considered insurmountable.

"Hayden?" It was Gracie, peering out the door of the camper at him. "What on earth are you doing out there all alone in the rain?"

"Moping," he admitted.

"Well, you just get yourself back inside this minute. All the moping in the world isn't going to make that sun shine again, and you know it."

So she thought his blue mood had resulted from the weather. For just a second Hayden wondered if he should share the real reason for it—namely his reservations about Tess. It wouldn't hurt to warn Gracie to guard her tongue, he thought as he stood and headed for the camper. After all, it had been a long time since a reporter darkened their door.

But no, he decided when he reached his aunt, who smiled at him as though she hadn't a care in the world. Gracie was blissfully ignorant of Tess's connection to their past. Therefore, meeting her had not resurrected any unpleasant memories. Why spoil her peace of mind?

Hopefully, all his suspicions were unfounded anyway. And even if they weren't and Tess somehow found an opportunity to ask his aunt questions about Sharon and Wade, Gracie surely knew better than to answer them. Heaven knew he'd harped on *that* enough.

"Here you go," Tess murmured, setting a saucer of cat food on her kitchen floor. Her smoky gray feline, Tabitha, walked nonchalantly to the dish, sniffed it, then sat without taking a bite, her opalescent green eyes raised accusingly to Tess.

"Expecting something else, were you?" Tess laughed and shook her head. "Sorry, Tabby. The bass filets are for dinner tomorrow night—*my* dinner."

That said, Tess surveyed her freshly cleaned kitchen with a critical eye, then walked to the living room, where her favorite rocking chair waited.

She sank into it with a sigh of weariness and reached automatically for the remote control. With a push of her finger, she turned on the television to watch the news. Instantly, a woman's voice, clear and polished, emanated from the set, reaching every corner of the tastefully furnished room. One by one, this or that well-spoken reporter shared the day's headlines, complete with on-location interviews.

Tess closed her eyes, trying to picture herself in their shoes, calmly describing a three-car pileup or questioning some poor robbery victim. Her stomach knotted at the very idea.

She thought back to her morning with Hayden and wondered again at her relief that he didn't want to talk about his personal life. A good reporter would never have given up so easily, she knew. Could it be that J.Q. was right after all? That she was nothing more than society editor material, famous father or no?

And if so, what would that father say?

Tess sighed, knowing that while Frank wouldn't *say* anything, he would definitely be disappointed. So much, in fact, that their close relationship might be threatened.

Her parents' divorce and a subsequent move to Arkansas from Illinois at age fifteen had strained relations with him once before. For well over a year Tess and her father communicated only on holidays or birthdays and then by telephone. She still cringed when she remembered those stilted conversations. They might as well have been strangers, a situation that actually worsened when her father suddenly remarried during Tess's senior year of high school.

In a desperate bid for his attention, she'd sent him a notebook of poems written in English class. To her astonishment, everything changed the moment Frank read them. Not only did he call that night, he called at least once a week thereafter—brimming with enthusiasm, full of advice on how to turn her writing talent into a career.

In short, they were pals once more.

And not for anything would Tess risk losing her beloved parent again, especially now that her mother had remarried to an old childhood beau and moved back to Europe.

No, not for anything....

But what about any*one?* In particular, a certain fisherman and his daughter, both of whom had already found a home in her heart?

Tess frowned, at once confused again. Deep inside, she knew she could never hurt Hayden and Savannah...even at the possible price of a career in reporting. Amazed by her conviction—already so strong, so sure—Tess wondered anew if she had what it took to succeed in the newspaper business.

She could only hope her hesitation stemmed from something else altogether: her unfortunate attraction to Hayden, the first and only person to ever make her doubt her career choice.

Tess arrived early at the lake on Wednesday morning so she could buy a fishing license at one of the local bait shops. That accomplished, she carried her bag, her life jacket, her rod and an ice chest packed with lunch and cold drinks to the boat-launching area.

The eastern horizon glowed coral and indigo by the time she reached the water's edge. Tess saw not one cloud in the sky and took pleasure in watching the rising sun, a glorious ball of red-orange flame that chased the early morning chill.

At six-fifteen, she saw Hayden get in his truck and drive it the short distance to the dock. He backed the trailer into the lake, then stepped out of the truck. His gaze swept Tess from head to toe, taking solemn note of her attire—white shorts, pink pullover top, matching socks, tennis shoes. Then he spotted her rod and reel.

"Going to do some fishing of your own today?" He sounded surprised.

"You bet," she told him, adding, "if you don't mind."

"Why would I mind?" That said, he made short work of loading and launching the bass boat. Tess moved the truck as before, and in minutes they sped across the lake.

She noted that Hayden headed in a different direction today, no doubt to explore new areas. Other boats dotted the lake. As Hayden guided his past them, he waved or nodded to each. Tess assumed they, too, were tournament participants testing the waters.

Finally they made their first stop. While Hayden killed the motor and picked up one of the rods and reels neatly stored in a rack along the side of the boat, Tess retrieved a tape recorder from her bag. After checking for proper loading of the audiocassette, she turned on the machine, set it in the seat and stepped up onto the back casting deck, rod in hand.

Once settled on the pedestal seat mounted there, she glanced over to Hayden, similarly situated and looking just too wonderful in snug-fitting jeans, deck shoes and a purple knit sport shirt. She noticed that he'd lowered the trolling motor into the water and now placed his foot on the control so he could utilize the motor as needed to keep the boat from drifting.

"Today I'd like to ask a few questions about your past tournament experiences and your technique," she said to him as he made his first cast. "Does that sound okay to you?"

"Sounds fine." He never took his eyes off his line, just began reeling it in.

Tess wondered at his manner—so cool, so reserved. It was almost as though he'd had second thoughts about inviting her along today. Not sure why he'd changed his mind, she made a quick cast and then got right down to business by asking about his years as a fishing guide, a question she'd thought of while lying wide-eyed and wide-awake at 2:00 a.m. that morning. No longer under the influence of Hayden's killer smile, she'd remembered quite a few questions that were really rather critical to her story.

"Actually I've been a guide since I first turned twenty," he told her. "Except for six or seven months about three years ago, that is. Then I worked in the fishing-tackle department of a sporting-goods chain in Texas."

"In Texas, huh? How'd you like it?"

"The state or the job?"

"Both."

"Texas is big and beautiful," he said. "I still have a house there, where Gracie, Savannah and I spend our winters. As for the job...I hated it, just like I knew I would."

"Then why on earth did you take it?" Tess blurted, without thought.

He hesitated, obviously on his guard. "I thought that the change, both in location and profession, might be the solution to some, uh, problems."

Suddenly certain that Hayden's problems were marital, thus providing her with a perfect lead-in to questions about his ex-wife, Tess found last night's conviction stood firm. She could not, would not jeopardize their friendship just to satisfy the curiosity of the public.

"What's the best bait for a lake like this, Hayden Bogart?"

He blinked in surprise at the sudden change in subject. "The best...? Oh, uh, well, that depends."

"On what? Lake conditions?"

"No," he replied quite seriously. "On when this story is coming out. Can't be telling my secrets *before* the tournament is over."

Tess had to laugh. "Actually, it should be in Friday evening's edition of the *Journal*."

"In that case, I'll have to pass on that particular question. Ask me another."

"Okay." She lifted her rod, checked her own favorite bait, then cast again. "Uh...tell me about your strategy."

He frowned, clearly giving this question serious consideration. "I plan to leave early every morning and get back in time for weigh-in every night."

With a soft snort of exasperation, Tess reeled in the rest of her line, laid the rod across her knees and swiveled the seat so she faced Hayden. Intent on checking his line, he didn't at first notice that she'd stopped fishing.

When he did look up, his eyes widened in feigned surprise. "Whasamatter?" he asked her, though she suspected he knew good and darn well.

"I can hardly report *that* as your strategy."

"Okay, okay," he retorted. "How about this? I'll leave early every morning, fish my favorite spots with my favorite baits and *then* get back to the dock in time for weigh-in."

"Oh, for—!" Tess heaved a lusty sigh. "Never mind. Tell me a little something about the habits of the large-mouth bass."

"Now there's a good safe topic," Hayden agreed. He then expounded at length, not only the habits of the species—about which he obviously knew a great deal— but on a few of the other factors that impacted on "fisherman's luck"—habitat and weather conditions among them.

He also talked about safety, boats, equipment and his favorite lakes. Tess listened intently, all the while fishing. Though she caught only one small bass for her efforts during the ensuing hours, Hayden caught several, each of which he set free with a friendly, *"Hasta la vista."*

Tess tried not to laugh at this rather eccentric behavior, but must have done something to give her amusement away. Suddenly she found herself the object of Hayden's attention.

"What's so funny?" he demanded.

"Well—" she shrugged rather self-consciously "—you're talking to the fish."

"So?"

"So don't you think that's a rather...peculiar thing to do?"

"Heck no," he replied. "I know of a fisherman who *kisses* every fish he catches."

Her jaw dropped. "You're lying."

"I'm not. I swear."

"But why would he do such a thing?"

"So his wife will believe that he's really been fishing all day," Hayden explained, completely straight-faced.

Tess digested that shocker, then bubbled with laughter in which her handsome companion soon joined.

The mood seemed to change after that, Tess thought. Hayden actually relaxed a bit and, if his frequent smiles and warm laughter were any indication, enjoyed himself.

Tess enjoyed herself, too, and was very surprised when Hayden glanced at his watch sometime after and said, "It's only ten-thirty, but I didn't have any breakfast and I'm starved. How do you feel about our finding a shade tree so we can eat a bite?"

"Is it really that late?" she exclaimed, startled in spite of the fact that she was on her fourth audiocassette.

He nodded.

"Then we'd certainly better eat. I have to go home, shower and change and be at work by one o'clock for a staff meeting." She turned off the recorder, stashed the tape along with the others in her purse and seated herself on the cushioned vinyl seat.

Instead of joining her and starting up the powerful motor mounted on the back of the boat, Hayden made use of the trolling motor. Slowly but surely, they glided nearer to the grassy bank. When the vessel nudged it, Hayden turned off the motor and leapt ashore. He then motioned for Tess to join him.

She grabbed her bag and moved toward the front of the boat, where she accepted his assistance in disembarking. Once she stood among the ankle-high wildflowers, Hayden climbed aboard the boat again and retrieved the ice chest. They walked together the few feet to the nearest shade, a towering oak.

From out of her bag Tess pulled a folded tablecloth, which she shook out and spread on the grass. She dropped to her knees at the edge of it and pushed back the handle of the ice chest so she could unpack. Then she motioned for Hayden to sit beside her.

Since she hadn't breakfasted, either, silence reigned for several minutes when they finally dug into the ham sandwiches she'd brought. She marveled that he ate two in the time it took her to eat half of one. He even chased them down with a couple of dill pickles, some potato chips and a cola.

His lunch finished, Hayden pushed his empty plate back and stretched out on his side inches from where she sat, her legs crossed Indian-style. Chin propped in his hand, he watched in silence as Tess munched on her pickle...or tried to. At once, she felt as awkward as a teenager and could barely swallow.

"Isn't it a beautiful day?" she blurted, to break what had become a weighty silence.

"Uh-huh,' he agreed without taking his dark eyes off her.

Tess opened her mouth to take another bite but found she couldn't, and so she lay down the pickle. She searched for something else to say—something clever—and, when nothing came to mind, self-consciously swiped at one of the gnats crashing their picnic.

It flew away, only to be replaced by several more, one of which was particularly pesky. Tess swatted and swatted again, then gasped and slapped a hand to her chest, just over her heart.

"That bug flew right down my top!" she exclaimed thoughtlessly.

"If I were a bug, that's where I'd fly," Hayden drawled, words that further disconcerted Tess.

Hastily she began to gather up the remains of their lunch, stuffing them haphazardly into the trash bag. Since she purposefully avoided Hayden's gaze, she jumped when he reached out and captured her right hand in his.

"I'm very sorry," he said. "I don't know why I said that. I hope I didn't embarrass you."

"I'm not embarrassed," Tess lied with a little laugh that sounded unconvincing even to her own ears. Quickly she freed her hand and changed the subject. "Did you get enough to eat?"

"More than enough, and it was delicious." He sat up, a move that put him right at her elbow. "You're a darn good cook."

"Thanks," she replied, flattered even though he didn't know what he was talking about. How could he when they'd lunched on cold sandwiches?

"A good fisherman, too."

Now that *was* a compliment. "Thanks, again."

"Do you mind if I ask a couple of questions?"

"What kind of questions?" she asked, a little distracted by the velvety softness of his faded blue jeans brushing her bare leg. "The kind I told you not to ask," he replied with a guilty grin. "The personal kind."

Tess hesitated, then shrugged. "I guess I don't mind. I mean, you have been very helpful, and I can always plead the fifth...."

He nodded. "First, I want to know why some hungry fisherman hasn't snatched you up. I mean it's not every woman who can cook *and* fish. And you're so beautiful...."

Tess waved away that foolishness. "Beautiful? Never. Pretty? Maybe, when I work at it. As for my being snatched... no way, Jose. I've got a career ladder to climb." She turned her head and found herself eye-to-eye with him. "I don't have time for marriage. I don't even have time for romance. Now what's your other question?"

"Actually, you just answered it," Hayden muttered, clearly disgruntled about something. He suddenly got to his feet and began to brush off his jeans.

Baffled, Tess tipped her head back to look up at him. She had to shade her eyes against the sun shining high overhead. "I did?"

"You did." He walked a few steps to a knoll that overlooked the lake. Tess jumped up and hurried after him.

"But what was it?" she persisted, intrigued.

"Nothing. Just forget it."

"I can't." Curiosity now had the better of her. "Tell me, Hayden... *please?*" She gave him her most winning smile... the one that usually always worked.

It worked again. "I was just going to ask if I could kiss you . . . okay?" The last word was almost a growl.

Tess caught her breath, then blurted, "Okay." When he didn't move or otherwise acknowledge her reply, she reached out and tugged on his sleeve. "I said 'okay,' Hayden. *O-kay.*"

Visibly perplexed, he said nothing for a second. Then his eyes widened. "You mean . . . ? Does that . . . ? May I . . . ?"

"For pity's sake," Tess exclaimed with a puff of impatience, throwing her arms around his neck. In a heartbeat, she tugged his face within reach and pressed her lips to his. "Now doesn't that beat the heck out of kissing some slimy old fish?" she teased when she released him a second later.

Instead of replying, Hayden caught Tess up in a bone-crushing embrace and initiated a kiss of his own. Her heels came up off the ground. The earth tipped; the heavens whirled; her heart kicked painfully and then thudded like crazy against her ribs.

Groaning softly, Hayden lifted her even higher. Tess heard nothing but his ragged breath—felt nothing but his powerful arms, wrapped so wonderfully, tightly across her waist and thighs.

Man, oh, man, she thought.

Suddenly Hayden dropped his head back. "Man, oh, man," he gasped to the heavens above.

Seconds ticked by. Hayden did not release Tess. She did not try to get away. Neither spoke. Then, with a lusty sigh that could have meant anything, he set her firmly on her feet again.

"You have to be at work by one o'clock," he said, a slight huskiness in his voice the only indication that something out of the ordinary had just taken place. "Any more of this, and you won't make it."

Struggling not to reveal her disappointment, Tess turned away. When she stooped over to finish gathering up the picnic things, she heard another deep groan, then found herself hauled into Hayden's arms again.

The kiss was different this time—longer, wetter, wilder. Better. Lost in sensation, Tess clung to Hayden, who sank to his knees, taking her with him. He then rolled onto his back, a move that pulled Tess full on top of him.

Not for an instant did he break the kiss. Instead, he actually deepened it, teasing her lips apart with his tongue so he could explore the interior of her mouth.

Tess savored the taste of him, so male, so uniquely Hayden Bogart, then did a little exploring of her own... and not just with her tongue. Her hands, too, were busy, unbuttoning a few buttons on his shirt. And when she finally raised her lips from his, it was just so she could touch them to the pulse pounding in his neck.

For the third time, Hayden groaned, a sexy sound that shimmied right down her spine. Without warning, he turned Tess on her back and sprawled over her, dropping hot, hungry kisses on her eyes, cheeks and chin.

Lost to his mastery, she forgot place and time....

But not for long. Suddenly a *beep, beep, beep* sounded from somewhere behind Hayden's head. At first Tess didn't even hear it. Then, when she heard it, she couldn't quite place it. She was that caught up.

Hayden shifted and raised up to take his weight on his elbows. He reached behind his neck and captured her wrist, pulling it down to peer at the source of the beeping—her wristwatch. "What in blue blazes is—"

"Oh my gosh!" Tess exclaimed, when she saw the watch. Hard hit by reality, she pushed Hayden aside and scrambled to her feet. "It's noon. I have to go." Impatiently she yanked at the tablecloth on which he still lay. As though her words had just sunk in, he jackknifed to his feet and snatched up the rest of the picnic things. A minute later they climbed aboard the boat. Two minutes after that, Hayden started the motor and guided the vessel away from their haven.

Tess thanked her lucky stars that the roar of the motor made speech impossible during the trip back to the dock. Still in shock from what had just transpired, she couldn't have managed normal conversation if she'd tried.

Time and again, she wondered what would have happened if the alarm hadn't sounded. Would they now be lying side by side on the secluded knoll, making slow, sweet love to each other?

Probably, she realized—an honest admission that brought the heat of shame to her cheeks.

Never one to take sex lightly, Tess had heretofore resisted any temptation to experiment. That was before she met Hayden, of course, a man for whom she still ached. A man with whom she would welcome an afternoon fling.

Fling? Most definitely. Neither Tess nor Hayden had energy, time or inclination for a relationship more lasting.

At that moment, the launching area came into view. Hayden immediately slowed the boat. Moments later, they closed the remaining distance to the ramp.

Tess noted that people milled all about. Clearly, she and Hayden would have to say a very public goodbye. Regret, immediate and intense, flooded her, and she realized with dismay that in spite of everything, she'd hoped for another kiss. Or two.

Damn.

Hayden, well used to the docking routine, soon stood at the nose of the boat, waiting to help Tess to solid ground. At his feet lay her life vest, ice chest and rod.

"I had a wonderful time, Hayden," she said when she stood beside him, her bag suspended from her shoulder by a strap. "Thanks for everything."

"You're very welcome," he replied, as formally as she. "You've got enough material, you think?"

"I have enough," she told him with honest regret. "Except for a brief follow-up interview after you win on Sunday, of course."

He chuckled at her prediction. They exchanged a polite smile—one that any two strangers would feel comfortable sharing. To Tess's amazement, her eyes stung and actually brimmed with what could only be disappointment. Embarrassed by the overreaction, she reached for her things.

"I'll get those," Hayden said, touching her arm to stop her.

"Not this time," Tess told him, quickly tucking the vest under one arm and then packing up the rod and ice chest in the other. "You'd better get back out there." Purposefully avoiding his gaze, she inclined her head toward the lake, sparkling crystal blue in the noonday sun.

"Well, if you're sure..."

Since he sounded as awkward as Tess felt, she made herself look at him. "I'm sure. Good luck, Hayden."

"Thanks." Their gazes locked. His was so cold that if his shirt hadn't still been unbuttoned to midchest Tess would actually have doubted the reality of their kisses.

Then he dropped his gaze to her mouth.

His expression did not change. He said nothing. But in his dark eyes flamed unmistakable desire—desire for her; desire that was no dream. Tess caught her breath, and pivoting away from him, ran like hell for her car.

Chapter Five

"Miss Tess?"

Intent on escape, Tess didn't at first hear the small voice calling out to her.

"Miss Tess!"

Abruptly Tess halted, mere feet from the haven of her vehicle. She glanced over the top of it toward Hayden's camper and immediately spotted Savannah, playing dolls at a nearby picnic table. Tess waved, and after loading her paraphernalia into her car, walked a few yards to the child. "Hi, there."

"Hi."

"I've been out with your dad," Tess told her. "If you look real quick, you might be able to see him—" She glanced back toward the dock, only belatedly wondering how Savannah would react to having Hayden come ashore without walking over to see her. "Oops, he's already gone back out." She gave the child an apologetic smile and tried to explain. "He still had a lot of practicing to do."

Savannah just shrugged, clearly used to her father's fishing habits.

"What's her name?" Tess asked to change the subject. She pointed to the baby doll in Savannah's arms.

"Roberta Elizabeth."

"Are you her mommy?"

Savannah huffed her disdain of such a stupid question. "I'm her big sister. We don't have a mommy."

"Oh," Tess said, at once saddened by that reply, uttered so coolly, so matter-of-factly. "Do you wish you did?"

"No" came the rather impatient reply. "And neither does my daddy. Roberta Elizabeth and me take real good care of him."

Before Tess could respond, Gracie rounded the corner of the camper, a paperback book and a folded-up lawn chair in hand.

"Why, hello," the woman said to her, adding a smile of genuine welcome. "I didn't know you were here."

"Only for a second," Tess told her. "I have to be at work in—" she glanced at her watch and winced "—thirty minutes."

"Goodness gracious. How far do you have to drive?"

Tess laughed at her startled expression. "Actually my office is only ten minutes away. I do have to stop off at my place on the way, though, to change clothes. My boss is pretty casual, but I think this—" she indicated her sporty attire "—might be a bit much even for him."

Gracie smiled again at her reply—a smile that looked a bit strained on closer inspection. At once, Tess took note of the woman's color—rather pale—and her eyes—decidedly lackluster.

"Are you feeling okay?" Tess asked, instantly concerned.

"Actually I have a humdinger of a sinus headache," Gracie told her as she set up the lawn chair in the shade of a tall pine tree. "I get them every time we come to Arkansas in the summer. Some kind of allergy, I expect."

"Will you two be all right until Hayden gets back?" Tess then asked.

"Oh, sure we will. I'm not going to do a thing but sit here and read. Hayden made a pot of chili at midnight last night—said he couldn't sleep—so I don't have to cook dinner."

"Yuck," Savannah suddenly announced from the picnic table where she still sat.

Biting back a laugh, Tess turned to her. "You don't like your daddy's chili?"

Savannah shook her head very emphatically. "It has onions and peppers in it." She wrinkled her nose with distaste.

At once an idea sprang to Tess's mind—an idea so bold that it definitely merited serious consideration before implementation.

"Then why don't the three of you come to my house for dinner?" she nonetheless blurted, not for the first time listening to her heart and not her head. "I'm cooking the fish Hayden and I caught yesterday."

At once Savannah's eyes lit up.

So did Gracie's, but then she shook her head. "I don't see how we can. Hayden said he planned to stay out on the lake until dark and then meet with some fellow contestants. There's just no telling how late he'll be. Fishermen do love to swap stories—"

"We could go without him," Savannah interjected. She quickly added, "He wouldn't care."

"I'm not so sure about that," Gracie replied with a look of censure.

"But Roberta Elizabeth wants to eat fish," Savannah whined.

"And I want to cook them for her," Tess said. She turned to Gracie. "How would you feel about my bringing everything over here to prepare? That way we can eat whenever we get ready and Hayden can have the leftovers."

"But that's so much trouble for you...."

"I don't mind a bit," Tess assured her, excited at the possibility of getting to know Hayden's family better.

Still Gracie hesitated, clearly in a quandary.

"I'll help her," Savannah promised in her grown-up way. She then immediately added a not-so-grown up "Please, please, pretty please?"

Gracie chuckled at that. "Oh, all right. Heaven knows, I wouldn't mind fish, myself. And I could certainly do with a little adult conversation to go with it."

"That settles it, then," Tess said. "I get off work at five and can be here by six-thirty. How does that sound?"

Gracie smiled. "Just wonderful, my dear. Just wonderful."

* * *

The clock on the paneled wall said 1:03 when Tess sailed into the conference room and seated herself with her co-workers at the oblong wooden table.

She noted that one or two staff members, including J.Q., still hadn't made an appearance—something on which she'd been counting—and sent heavenward a silent thank-you. She glanced down, making sure she hadn't forgotten to zip the khaki straight skirt into which she'd leapt mere minutes before, then straightened her pink pullover, the same one she'd worn that morning. She could only hope it—and *she*—didn't smell fishy. There simply hadn't been time for a shower as originally planned...not after she and Gracie worked out the details for dinner that night.

Dinner.

Tess still couldn't believe what she'd done. As for *why* she'd done it...well, that was no mystery at all. Not only did she really like Gracie and Savannah, she liked Hayden, too. In fact, she thrilled even now at the memory of his kiss and the predatory gleam in his eye when they parted barely an hour ago.

And though she knew she played with fire, she looked forward to seeing him again, being the object of his desire....

"Glad you all could make it this afternoon," boomed J.Q., a greeting that yanked Tess right out of her fantasy into the here and now. She quickly straightened in her chair and turned her attention to her boss, seated at the head of the table.

Steadfastly throughout the meeting, she kept her mind on the business at hand. It wasn't easy. J.Q. had a tendency to rehash old gripes. Today was no exception until he suddenly stood and slapped his hand to a poster, which he had earlier propped in an easel so everyone present could view it.

"What you see here are the results of a popularity poll taken by the *Arkansas Daily*. As you can see, the *Jenner Springs Journal* is listed as number three. *Number three.*" He jabbed at the chart, a gesture that indicated quite clearly that he was not a happy man.

"We've slipped!" he then roared, glaring at each of them in turn. When his glinting eyes found Tess, she squirmed in her chair and wondered for the umpteenth time that week if she had made a wise career choice. At the moment, another profession—any other profession—held more appeal.

"Now I'm going to go around this table," J.Q. continued. "And I want each of you to tell the others about your current project. We're going to put our heads together today. We're going to punch up these stories. We're going to raise ourselves back to number two on that damned popularity poll." He slapped the chart again. "Hell, we may even make number one before we're finished!"

Dead silence followed J.Q.'s prediction. Covertly, Tess scanned the faces in the room, noting a variety of expressions ranging from mild interest to excitement. On not one of them did she read the dread now chilling her to the bone.

As requested, each staff member described his or her assignment. After each came a brief period of brainstorming, during which co-workers offered suggestions. Tess said little. Instead, she worried how she would present her own project to this group without saying Hayden's name, which she believed J.Q. would immediately recognize.

"Tess? You're assigned to the fishing tournament on Miller Lake, aren't you?"

She jumped rather guiltily at J.Q.'s question, then cleared her throat. "Yes."

"Tell us your angle."

Tess swallowed hard. "Since there has been so much controversy and bad press about the tournament, I thought I'd present the fisherman's side of the issue."

"And how are you going to do that?"

"I'm interviewing one of the participants," Tess hedged.

"Which one?" asked Bo Braden, another reporter hopeful and an avid fishing enthusiast.

Tess hesitated only fractionally before giving in to the inevitable. "Hayden Bogart. I thought I'd do a personal profile for Friday's edition, report his ABFA tournament standing on Monday, after this weekend's competition is over, and, if he makes it to the Super-tourney, do a follow-up story later."

With bated breath, she waited for the reaction to her bombshell. There was none. Even from J.Q. It was all Tess could do not to heave a massive sigh of relief. Clearly her own guilty conscience had made this interview a much bigger deal than it really was. Nobody remembered Hayden Bogart, much less connected him to Wade Waterson. All her worries had been for naught.

The meeting lasted only another half hour after that. Anxious to get back to her desk and the society editor work she had as good as neglected while on the lake for the past two days, Tess hurried from the room and headed to her office.

"Tess?" It was J.Q. . . . and hard on her heels.

She stopped short and slowly turned. "Yes, sir?"

"Can you come into my office for a minute?" Not waiting for an answer, he strode past and on down the hall. Heart in her throat, Tess followed with dragging steps. "Have a seat," he said when she walked through his door seconds later.

Tess did as requested.

"Did you say that you're interviewing Hayden Bogart?"

Tess tensed. "That's correct."

"You tried to interview him once before, I believe. About three years ago?"

Uh-oh, here it comes. "Yes."

"I seem to recall he wasn't very cooperative that first time. How's he doing now?"

"He . . . I . . . Actually, we're getting along just fine. I've spent the last two mornings with him out on his boat and—"

"That's where you were this morning? Out on the lake?"

Tess nodded.

"And yesterday, too?"

She nodded once more.

"When are you seeing him again?" J.Q. next asked.

Tess's stomach churned with anxiety. "Tonight." She noted an immediate spark of interest in her boss's eye and imagined the wheels of conjecture spinning in his brain.

"Have you mentioned Wade Waterson to him?" he asked, rather predictably, after a weighty silence.

"Well . . . no, I haven't."

"Why not?"

"I hated to resurrect painful memories."

"You're too softhearted, Tess," he scolded. "Those 'painful memories' could be tomorrow's headlines."

"But surely nobody's interested in that old story."

"Old, hell. You know that Waterson has announced his candidacy again. That story is as pertinent now as it was three years ago, and there are lots of people interested. Lots."

"Maybe so, but Hayden has already warned that he won't answer personal questions."

"And since when did that stop a serious reporter from doing her job?" J.Q. scooted his chair back and began to pace, something he always did when agitated. Suddenly he stopped and whirled on her. He pointed an accusing finger. "You *are* a serious reporter, aren't you?"

Tess, wondering the same thing, could barely reply. "I—I think so."

"You *think* so," he echoed, walking back to his chair to plop down in it with a heavy sigh. He rubbed his eyes as though they ached, then raised his gaze to meet hers. "Tess, I believe it's time for some straight talk. You're a talented writer. You're organized, dependable, hardworking. Unfortunately it takes more than that to succeed in this business. It takes guts and ruthless perseverance. Frankly, Tess, I've seen no indication that you have either of those qualities, and I'm beginning to wonder if I ever will."

Stunned, her hopes and dreams falling in a heap about her feet, Tess could not have replied if she wanted.

"So I have a challenge for you," J.Q. continued, his expression actually softening somewhat. He rubbed his chin rather thoughtfully, all the while studying her. "Bring me back the truth about what happened between Sharon Bogart and Wade Waterson three years ago. Do that, and I'll know you've got what it takes. More important, *you'll* know it, too. Now go." He dismissed her with a wave. "Get out of here and *get that story.* I'm counting on you."

Tess mulled over J.Q.'s challenge until quitting time, when she abruptly concluded that he was right. Unequivocally.

If she were going to be a famous reporter—or even an *un*famous one—she would have to get over her squeamishness about prying into people's personal lives...starting with Hayden...starting tonight.

Unfortunately that decision, made with such determination at five o'clock, weighed heavily on Tess's mind by the time she drove back to Miller Lake, food in tow, at six-thirty and stopped her car next to Hayden's truck, boat and trailer, now parked near the camper. Gracie's warm greeting and Savannah's smile of welcome did not soothe her stricken conscience one whit.

Since Hayden was not home and Savannah had just had a snack of milk and cookies, Tess decided not to start dinner right away. Instead, she sat by Gracie and Savannah on the couch and listened to the silver-haired woman talk about everything from last year's family reunion—a cousin believed to be long dead had shown up—to that summer's movie releases—wasn't that good-looking actor what'sisname starring in one of them?

Seven o'clock came and went without an appearance by Hayden, as did seven-thirty. Gracie chatted without ceasing, a fact that only increased Tess's guilt since she suspected Hayden's lonely aunt would gladly answer any question asked of her—even personal ones—thereby obviating the need to interview Hayden again. So why did Tess avoid such questions? Why didn't she just ask Gracie all about Sharon? And about Wade?

And why was she so very glad when Savannah suddenly announced, "Roberta Elizabeth wants to eat *now.*"

Not even attempting to find answers for her dilemma, Tess gladly jumped right to her feet and got busy in Gracie's kitchen. The meal, consisting of fish, corn on the cob and salad, did not take long to prepare and the three of them soon sat down at the table.

Tess couldn't help but glance toward the door more than once, half expecting Hayden to burst through it at any moment. As though reading her thoughts, Gracie smiled and patted her hand.

"Don't worry, dear. I'm sure he'll be here before long. He's with the other contestants right now. They're all old fishing buddies, you know, and concerned about how the weather has affected the fishing."

"Oh, I'm not worried," Tess murmured, a little embarrassed that Gracie had misread her restlessness. In actuality, Tess was almost glad Hayden hadn't come home. If she didn't see him tonight, she couldn't ask the questions J.Q. wanted answered.

At nine, Gracie dressed Savannah in a Barbie nightshirt and tucked her into the bunk bed over their heads.

That arrangement lasted maybe fifteen minutes before the girl hung down over them and suggested a game of Candy Land, an idea immediately vetoed by Gracie.

"I can't imagine what's wrong with that child tonight," the woman exclaimed after tucking in her niece twice more. "I've let her stay up half an hour past her bedtime already. She's bound to be sleepy."

At once, Tess noted the dark lines of weariness under Gracie's eyes and guessed Savannah wasn't the only one with an early bedtime. "It's my fault. In fact, I'm keeping you both up, aren't I?" She, too, stood. "I think I'd better just go on home...."

"Oh, no," Gracie argued, visibly distressed. "You can't leave before Hayden gets back. Why, he'd never forgive me."

He wouldn't? "But you're obviously tired, and Savannah isn't going to stay down as long as I'm here."

"And probably not even if you leave," Gracie replied. "Please wait for Hayden."

Tess hesitated, then shrugged. "Okay, *if* you'll go on to bed."

"But I—"

"No buts. I can tell you're exhausted. I'll watch Savannah for you."

Clearly torn between playing hostess and getting some sleep, Gracie didn't speak for a moment. Then she smiled with some relief. "Well, if you're sure you don't mind...."

"I don't mind a bit," Tess told her. She winked at Savannah. "In fact, I'm really looking forward to Candy Land." She laughed. "I haven't played in a good number of years. I'll probably slide when I should climb."

Savannah, already scrambling out of her bed, giggled. "That's not Candy Land, that's Chutes and Ladders."

"So it is," Tess agreed, joining in her laughter even as Gracie escaped to what must be her bedroom.

In minutes, Tess and a wide-awake Savannah sat at the table again, heads bent over a colorful gameboard. After the child's brief explanation of game rules, the two of them began to play.

Created for preschoolers, the game required little thought and less strategy. But Tess was never bored, thanks to Savannah's lively chatter.

"I'm going to kiddiegarter next year."

"Is that so?" Tess murmured, struggling not to smile.

Savannah nodded. "After kiddiegarter comes first grade...then college." She sounded book-weary already.

"And after college?"

"I'm going to get a job."

"Smart girl. What kind of job do you want?"

She thought for a moment. "I'm going to stand behind a glass box and spray perfume right here—" she pointed to her neck "—for men to smell when they walk by."

Tess blinked in surprise at Savannah's answer, so different from the "nurse" or "teacher" she'd expected. "And where do you get a job like that?"

"At the mall," Savannah informed her. "There's a lady there that does it. Daddy smelled her one time when me and him were shopping for Gracie a birthday present."

"I see." Tess marveled at the jealousy—the *ridiculous* jealousy—now stabbing at her. "Was she pretty?"

Savannah nodded. "Real pretty. She had on a shiny red blouse that came clear down to here." She touched her forefinger somewhere in the vicinity of her belly button.

"I see. Did your daddy buy the perfume?"

She nodded again, "And he gave it to Gracie. She don't wear it though."

"Why not?" Tess asked.

"It makes her sneeze."

Tess swallowed back her laugh. "Does it make you sneeze?"

"No," Savannah replied. "Want me to show you?"

"Maybe later."

Silence reigned for a moment—a *brief* moment—while Savannah advanced her player several colored squares.

"Do you like my daddy?" she then asked.

Tess tensed. "Why, yes."

"How much?"

"He's, um, a good friend."

"Is that the same thing as a boyfriend?"

"No," Tess replied with shocking regret.

Savannah's eyes locked with hers. "Good," she said, wrapping a strand of flame-red hair around her finger and absently twisting it.

"Why do you say that?" Tess asked, too intrigued to take the comment personally.

"'Cause my best friend, Emerald's daddy had a girlfriend one time and now she's a stepmother. I don't want a stepmother."

"Even if she could make your daddy happy?"

LUCKY STARS

Everybody's got a Lucky Star & this may be yours. SCRATCH GOLD FROM BOX & STAR. If both match, you're definitely in - you qualify for a chance to win the Super Bonus Prize revealed!

TE
Pri
Als
obl
rep

Nam

Stre

City

©19

SEPARATE AT DOTTED LINES — PLAY BOTH & RETURN IN REPLY

Extra

Super EXTRA DOUBLE BONUS BONUS PRIZE

Prizes on these Games are BONUS EXTRAS, all for 1 winner, AND on top of

You
not
nam
Sw
get
ter
any

Savannah shook her head so hard that her hair whipped her face.

"Why not?" Tess asked.

"Just look what happened to Cinderella," came the child's solemn reply.

Tess nearly choked. "But that was just a fairy tale. Most stepmothers are usually very nice people."

"How do you know?"

"I have one."

Savannah's eyes rounded. *"You do?"*

"I do, and I like her a lot."

"Cross your heart?"

"Cross my heart," Tess said, doing exactly that, a motion that clearly impressed her companion.

By the time the clock said ten-thirty, Savannah's eyes weren't so wide and conversation definitely lagged.

"Oh my goodness," Tess exclaimed when Savannah turned over a game card to reveal just the color she needed to advance her player safely past Molasses Swamp to King Kandy's castle. "You've won again! That makes you the grand champion." Quickly Tess cleared up the game pieces. "Are you sleepy yet?"

"No," Savannah replied, struggling to keep her droopy eyes open.

"Good. Want me to tell you about the time I flew my Uncle Kevin's airplane? I was just a couple of years older than you."

Savannah nodded eagerly.

"All right, but you'll have to get in your bed first."

Without hesitation, the redheaded moppet scooted out of the booth and walked over to the couch, where Roberta Elizabeth lay on a threadbare quilt. She scooped up both and, with a boost from Tess, climbed back into her bunk.

Since a cool night breeze blew through the screened windows, Tess covered Savannah with a sheet, then sat back down at the table and began to verbalize her favorite childhood memory. By the time she reached the part where her father's younger brother Kevin, a crop duster, offered to let her fly his plane, Savannah's eyes had closed.

Tess bit back a smile of satisfaction and continued her tale, certain that the child would fall asleep in less time than she had actually commandeered her Uncle Kevin's marvelous flying machine—three whole seconds.

"...And I remember how blue the sky was that day. There wasn't one single cloud..."

Startled to hear that familiar voice emanating so clearly through the windows of his camper, Hayden stopped short in the shadows outside. Just returning from being away for hours, he was naturally disturbed and a little suspicious to find Tess there with Savannah, whom he could see lying in her bed. Gracie was not in sight.

When and why had Tess come? he worried only fleetingly before a deeper, stronger emotion—namely joy—filled his heart.

Hayden gave in to that joy without a fight and stood silent in the dark just outside the window, relishing the cadence of Tess's silky Southern drawl. Though he could not actually see her from where he stood, all he had to do was close his eyes to remember how she'd looked that morning—breathtakingly lovely. At once he ached to hold her again.

"...Uncle Kevin flew us right over my house. It was so tiny...."

Barely registering Tess's story, related, no doubt, for his daughter's benefit, Hayden relived the kisses they'd shared. He smelled again the scent of Tess's perfume, tasted again her sweet, sweet lips. Lost to his memories, Hayden promptly forgot the bad weather—more rainstorms had been forecast—and his subsequent fishing woes.

He thought, instead, about leaving the lake and taking Tess someplace far away from reality where they would make love until his hunger was sated. How long would that take? he couldn't help but wonder.

Days? Weeks? Months? Years?

Forever?

At that moment, Tess stopped her story and stepped into Hayden's line of vision. She moved rather stealthily to smooth Savannah's cover, a sure sign that the child had succumbed to sleep.

Burning with desire, Hayden took immediate advantage of the situation by stepping boldly to the door. He yanked it open and reached inside to capture Tess's wrist in his hand. With a firm tug, he then pulled his startled guest right outside and into his waiting arms.

Holding her tightly, Hayden pivoted, sidestepped his truck and walked the few steps to the nearby picnic area, now cloaked in the privacy of deep shadow. When he sat Tess on the edge of the nearest tabletop something rolled off, landing with a soft plop in the grass. Before he could discover what it was, however, Tess distracted him by wrapping her legs around his

thighs and locking her ankles to hold him immobile—
a move that snapped his self-control.

Everything forgotten but the woman in his arms,
Hayden crushed Tess to him and kissed her again...and
again. Without thought, without hesitation, without
permission, he traced her curves with his hands.

Tess gasped when his thumb teased the peak of one
breast to tautness. Hayden instantly stopped his ex-
ploration, but she arched her back, urging him on, an
invitation he could not mistake or refuse. Groaning
softly in response, he took the weight of her breast in
his palm and placed a kiss on the soft knit top stretched
over it.

This time the groan slipped from Tess's lips. Both
hands tangled in his hair, she tipped her head back.
Hayden kissed her throat, then her cheek, chin and
mouth. She parted her lips for him. Their tongues
teased and tangled.

As she had earlier that day, Tess unbuttoned his shirt
without breaking their kiss. But this time she freed each
and every button and then pushed the garment back off
his shoulders. Hayden tensed when her fingernails
lightly raked his chest. He moaned when she lay her
cheek on his thudding heart.

"Ah, Tess," he growled. "What are you doing to
me?"

"Not as much as I want to," came her husky reply.

None too gently, Hayden covered her lips with his in
a hungry kiss. His hands were everywhere now, bolder
still, and Tess responded with abandon. Lost in the
magic of their lovemaking, which was everything he'd
dreamed it would be, Hayden untucked the hem of her

pullover top and slipped his hands underneath to caress her bare breasts.

Tess shuddered to his touch, and Hayden knew she wanted him as much as he wanted her. Instantly, he tried to think of somewhere they could go to be alone and finish what he—or was it she?—had started.

"Tess?"

From the sound of Savannah's cry, Hayden guessed she stood in the open doorway of the camper, most likely looking out. Though the tall pine trees blocked the light of the park's mercury vapor lamps, thus hiding them, Hayden stepped reflexively between Tess and his insomniac daughter. While Tess tucked her top back in, he fumbled with his buttons.

"I'll get them," he whispered, when she tried to help. He lifted her off the table. "You go on inside. I'll be there in a minute."

Without hesitation, Tess obeyed, squaring her shoulders, moving into the light streaming through the camper door.

"Just what are you doing out of bed, Miss Bogart?" she teased with remarkable normalcy considering she'd just crashed back to earth from paradise.

"Waiting for Daddy," Savannah replied, stepping back so Tess could enter the camper and then peering around her and out the door. "When's he coming in?"

Tess, still breathless from Hayden's skillful manhandling, cringed and imagined the worst, a disastrous scenario that struck her speechless and brought heat to her cheeks. "Oh, uh, he, uh—"

"Right this minute." Smooth as silk, Hayden stepped through the door and scooped up his pint-size daughter. "Hey there, kiddo. Whatcha been doing all day?" he asked, giving her a hug.

"Baby-sitting Roberta Elizabeth," she replied with a heavy sigh.

"Hmm. Has she been a good girl?"

"Pretty good."

"And what about you?"

"Me, too," Savannah replied.

"Except for staying up two hours after bedtime?" Hayden teased.

"Tess and I have been playing Candy Land," Savannah explained, adding, "Gracie has a headache so Tess cooked fish for our dinner. It was real good."

"Yeah?" *So that's what she was doing here.* Hayden smiled gratefully at Tess. "Thanks."

"My pleasure," Tess replied. "Yours is in the oven."

"Good. I'm starved." He took a step toward the bunk. "Time for bed, kiddo," he said to his daughter, who immediately began to squirm.

"But I haven't given Roberta Elizabeth her night bottle."

"Can't you do that in your bed?"

"No," Savannah informed him.

"And why not?"

"'Cause I don't have it."

Hayden looked all around. "Okay, Vanna. Where's the bottle? In the refrigerator?"

"No."

"The pantry?"

"No."

"The closet? The hamper? My tackle box?"

She giggled. "No, no, no."

"Then where?" He touched the tip of his nose to his daughter's and looked her dead in the eye. "And make it snappy. Time's a-wasting."

"Outside."

"What?"

"I left it on the picnic table. The one where you and Tess were sitting."

Tess gulped and met Hayden's gaze across the room, not sure what reaction to expect from him.

But he just murmured, "I believe I know right where it is," before tucking his red-haired pixie into her bed and exiting the camper.

Suddenly ill at ease, Tess smiled rather nervously at Savannah, whose bright eyes never left her. At once their conversation about good friends and boyfriends came to mind.

Had the child seen something that confused her? Tess wondered, blushing when she realized that could well be the case. At once she longed for escape from that very observant gaze.

"It's awfully late, isn't it?" Tess snatched up the bag into which she had packed her empty dishes. "I'd better go." She wiggled her fingers in a little wave to Savannah, then gave the child a friendly smile she hoped would restore her trust. "I had a really nice time."

"Me, too."

"I'm so glad." She moved toward the door, pausing before she exited the camper. "Good night, Savannah."

"Good night, sleep tight, don't let the bad bugs bite," Savannah solemnly advised.

Chapter Six

Bad bugs? Well, that did make sense. Tess bit back a grin and escaped into the cool of the night where she almost crashed into Hayden, just returning with a plastic dolly bottle in hand. Catching his arm, she practically dragged him back into the deep shadows adjacent to the camper.

"Do you think Savannah saw us?" Tess whispered even as she reassured herself to the contrary by glancing toward the picnic table. She could barely discern its shape in the dark.

"Saw us what?" Hayden asked.

"What do you think?"

Hayden chuckled and surprised Tess by stepping forward to pin her to the camper with his body. He then kissed her—long and hard—on the mouth.

"Doing that?" he asked when he finally raised his head.

"Exactly that," Tess squeaked, weak-kneed as usual, and welcoming the support of the trailer at her back.

"I doubt it, but what if she did?"

"I'd just die."

"Why?" he demanded, stepping back half a pace so he could look her in the eye, not an easy accomplishment in that scant light. "Don't tell me you're embarrassed."

"Not embarrassed. Worried."

"About what, for crying out loud?"

"Not a what, a *who*. Your daughter, who is rather possessive of you."

Hayden laughed outright. "Don't be ridiculous. Anyway, she likes you."

"Think so?" Tess asked, not so sure.

"Know so," he insisted. "And who can blame her? You're a great cook. You play a mean game of Candy Land—"

"Actually I lost three times."

"Ouch." Silence reined for a moment. "So forget Candy Land. You're a great cook, and you tell wonderful stories."

Tess arched an eyebrow in surprise. "I didn't realize you heard my story."

"I did, and I loved it." He pulled her close again. "Have you ever thought about writing for children?"

Tess tensed and pushed him away. "Still trying to change my profession?"

"No," he said with a shrug she felt more than saw, "but I am still trying to figure out why you ever chose it in the first place. I just can't imagine a sensitive, caring woman like you doing this sort of work forever."

"But I don't plan to do it forever, remember? I'm only working for the *Journal* because it's a vital step on my career ladder."

"You sound as though you're quoting someone when you say that," he commented.

"I am," Tess said. "My dad."

"He must be proud of you."

"Very."

"And supportive?"

"I'd never have made it through college without his help."

Another silence followed her reply. Then Hayden said, "May I give you a word of advice?"

"If you're going to suggest I find a new career, then the answer is no."

"Hey, what you do for a living is strictly your business. Not mine. *And not your dad's.*"

"What are you trying to say?" Tess demanded.

"That you'll never be happy if your career choice is based on a desire to please someone else." He frowned, as though lost in some unpleasant memories. "Trust me, Tess, I know. I've been there."

"The sporting-goods store in Texas?"

Hayden nodded.

At once, Tess's heart went out to him. "Don't worry about me. I know what I'm doing. Really. Now I need to go, and you need to eat."

"Speaking of eating, I promised Gracie and Savannah I'd take them to dinner at the Catch-N-Cook tomorrow night—"

"Fish *again?*"

"Savannah never gets tired of it," Hayden said.

"Neither do I," Tess admitted with a laugh.

"Good, because I want you to join us."

"Really?" Her spirits soared.

"Really. Gracie and Savannah would love it."

"Oh." So much for soaring spirits. "And what about you? Would you love it?"

"Me, most of all," he told her, a reply that took her breath and made those roller coaster spirits climb again. "Is seven okay?"

"Seven is perfect."

"I'll pick you up."

"No, I'll meet you all there."

"Then it's a date?"

A date? With two chaperons in tow? Tess couldn't keep from laughing.

"What's so funny?" Hayden demanded. The dim light streaming through the nearest window caught and magnified a dangerously sexy gleam in his dark eyes.

"Nothing," she told him, at once oh-so-thankful for those chaperons. "And yes, it's a date."

Thursday dragged by for Tess. Though secure in her decision not to mention anything of Hayden's traumatic past or Wade Waterson's political future in her article, she still dreaded J.Q.'s reaction.

For that reason, she did her best to avoid her boss all day by hiding behind her computer monitor and meticulously typing out her report.

With infinite care, she presented the fisherman's case—the pros of bass-fishing tournaments. There were many—among them, increased revenue for local merchants, nationwide exposure of her state's parks and lakes and public awareness of the ecologically sound catch-and-release program.

As for the cons...a little extra traffic and trash were hardly reason enough to ban the competitions. Tess stated that controversial point of view in no uncertain terms, too, and when she finally printed out the article and reread it late that afternoon, she felt pride in the final product.

The piece was good, if not exactly what J.Q. had asked for. Would he be so impressed that he would forgive her for failing him again? Would he let her do the other stories she wanted to do, and without further hassle?

Fat chance, she thought. More likely he would consider this article her resignation.

Unsure and unwilling to hang around and find out for sure which way J.Q. would react, Tess lay the completed report on his desk at quitting time and skedaddled right out the door to her car.

Tomorrow would be soon enough to face her boss. By then she might have the courage to speak out in her own defense. Heck, by then she might even be able to tell J.Q. the main reason why she hadn't pursued and printed the truth about Hayden's tragic past.

Heaven knows she couldn't do it now...probably because there wasn't any "main" reason. There were, however, some not-so-main ones, among them her reluctance to hurt Hayden and his family, as well as a little thing called integrity.

Laudable reasons, those, she thought. She could definitely hold her head high....

"Very high," Tess muttered aloud as she slipped behind the steering wheel of her car and inserted the key. "All the way to the employment office."

With a sigh, she started the engine and headed for home, her thoughts awhirl as she tried to envision the best and worst that could happen.

Without a doubt, the best would be a pat on the back from J.Q.

The worst? Why, losing her job, of course.

Or would that be the worst? Tess pulled into her drive and killed the engine, then sat immobile for a moment, trying to imagine working somewhere besides the *Journal*. It was surprisingly easy in spite of her years there, and closing her eyes, Tess let her thoughts run free.

Since she set no boundaries, several alternative jobs soon came to mind, all of them related to her degree and influenced by her love of the written word. Of those, one in particular held a great deal of appeal: teaching journalism.

Immediately Tess tried to picture herself in front of a classroom of teenagers. She found that scenario amazingly intriguing and belatedly remembered the journalism teacher who'd taught when she was a senior in high school. What fun they'd had working on the school newspaper and on the yearbook.

At once, other memories—happy memories—came to mind. Those memories triggered still more and suddenly Tess recalled a long-forgotten dream to be just like that very special teacher who'd made learning so much fun.

Oddly wistful, wondering how she could have forgotten so completely what was once a burning desire, Tess came to life rather abruptly and got out of her car. As she walked to her porch, a new emotion—guilt—took control.

"Now don't get yourself in a dither about finding a new job," Tess scolded aloud as she unlocked the front door. "You can always be society editor somewhere."

A second later, she stepped inside to get ready for her "date"—an event that *did* merit some serious dithering.

Seven o'clock found Tess at the Catch-N-Cook. When a quick peek inside revealed that Hayden and Co. had not yet arrived, she settled herself in one of the grapevine chairs out on the covered porch that stretched from one end of the rugged log structure to the other.

A cool, moist breeze fanned her face and hair and sent chill bumps dancing down her bare arms. Tess couldn't help but wonder if she should've worn something warmer than this tropical print sundress with its tiny straps, even if it was her favorite outfit.

Moments later, when her dinner companions showed up, she decided her decision was the right one after all... at least if the look on Hayden's face was anything to go by.

While Gracie and Savannah greeted Tess, Hayden gave her a twice over that started at her bangs, U-turned at her sandaled feet and then traveled back up to her mouth, where it seemed to stall. Tess felt quite... *touched*... by the time he raised his gaze enough to lock with hers.

Cheeks burning, body atingle, lips craving the marvelously male taste of his, now curved in a sexy smile, she spoke in what she hoped was a normal voice. "Hello, Hayden."

"Hello."

He said nothing else; he just looked at her as though weeks and not mere hours had passed since he'd seen her...as though they had done much more than just kiss, the last time they were together.

Tess squirmed under that look and prayed that Gracie and Savannah didn't notice his distraction or the awkward silence.

"Are we going to eat, or just stand here?" Savannah suddenly demanded, much to Tess's relief.

"Eat," Hayden told his daughter. He reached out and pulled open the ornate log door. "Redheads first."

Giggling, Savannah sashayed inside. Gracie looked from Hayden to Tess, smiled sweetly, then followed. When Tess moved to do the same, Hayden stepped quickly in front of her, his hand on the door handle. In a move so smooth no one could have noticed, he pushed the door nearly shut, kissed Tess full on the mouth, then took her arm and hustled her on into the restaurant.

Tess blinked against the bright lights, and she promptly tripped.

"You okay?" Hayden asked, tightening his hold on her.

"Fine," she replied, as annoyed with him for catching her off guard as with herself for reacting like such a ninny. It wasn't as though she was sweet sixteen and had never been kissed, for heaven's sake. Abruptly Tess reigned in her runaway emotions and slipped free of Hayden. "Have you ever eaten here before?" she turned to ask Gracie.

"No," the woman replied.

"Then you haven't met Rodney Spencer?"

"Who?"

"Rodney Spencer, otherwise known as Fishbait, owner of this restaurant." Tess pointed to the window that separated the dining from the cooking area. Just visible through it was the man in question, working with his back to them.

"I don't know him," Gracie said, her gaze on Fishbait.

Tess smiled. "Then I'll call him out in a bit, but I think it only fair to warn you that he's a sweet-talking bachelor with an eye for a pretty lady."

Gracie sputtered her embarrassment at the compliment and waved it away. Tess noted with approval the blush on her cheek and the sparkle in her eye.

"Can we sit over there?" Savannah asked at that moment, pointing to a table near the windows.

"It's all right with me," Tess told her. "But before we sit down, we have to get our dinner from that buffet over there."

Savannah looked toward the impressively long food line. Immediately her eyes lit up. Grabbing Tess's hand, she headed that way. Hayden and Gracie followed.

It didn't take Tess or Savannah long to select from the piping hot menu items what they wanted to eat. Then they walked together to the table the child had earlier picked out and sat opposite one another. When a waitress appeared to take their drink orders, Tess glanced toward the buffet, where Hayden and Gracie still stood, apparently waiting on a fresh-fried batch of something or other.

Tess therefore requested iced tea for herself and chocolate milk for her companion, then instructed the waitress to check back in a few moments for the other two orders.

"I'm glad you came with us," Savannah said the moment they were alone again.

"Why, thank you," Tess said. Then she added, "You look very pretty in that yellow dress. Did you pick it out yourself?"

"No," Savannah said. "It was a surprise from my daddy." She glanced quickly toward her dad and Gracie, still at the buffet. "Are you going to kiss him again tonight?"

Tess caught her breath, shocked that the child, and no telling who else, had witnessed that quick kiss with which Hayden had gifted her moments ago. "Again?"

"I saw you kissing on the picnic table."

Great. "You saw me kissing the picnic table?" Tess asked, in a bid for time and, she hoped, inspiration. An expert with four-year-olds Tess was not.

"No, silly," Savannah replied with a huff of exasperation. "I saw you sitting on the picnic table, kissing my daddy. Now are you going to do it again or not?"

Tess swallowed hard and welcomed the reappearance of the waitress with their drinks. All too soon, she and Savannah were alone once more, but by then Tess knew what to reply. "Ask your daddy."

Savannah sighed. "I did already."

"*Oh?* And what did he say?"

"He said that you would."

"She would what?"

Tess almost fell out of her chair at the sound of Hayden's voice, so close behind her.

"Kiss you again," Savannah replied as though she discussed such things at every meal.

"Oh," her dad replied with equal aplomb. He sat down next to Tess. "And will you mind if she does?" he asked the question of Savannah, but his eyes were on Tess. So were Gracie's, and Tess squirmed in response to their scrutiny.

"No," Savannah told him, at which point Hayden gave Tess an I-told-you-so nod. "I've decided that taking care of you is too much sponsibility for me and Roberta Elizabeth. We're very young, you know."

The corners of Hayden's mouth twitched, but he didn't smile. "I know."

"And all the stepmothers aren't like Cinderella's," Savannah continued, a comment that obviously startled her father, whose full attention she now had. Tess watched the color drain from his face.

"Did you say—" he gulped audibly "—stepmothers?"

Savannah nodded. "Some of them are nice. Tess told me so."

Once more, Tess found herself on the receiving end of Hayden's gaze. He looked rather disconcerted, no, downright wary...and no wonder. He probably thought she'd been brainwashing his offspring. How embarrassing.

"Will you please pass the ketchup," Tess said to Savannah in an attempt to change the topic of conversation.

Savannah did as requested, then had to pass the salt and pepper to Gracie. At that moment, the waitress appeared again and took the other two drink orders.

Normalcy returned with the delivery of those drinks. Deliberately, Tess kept the conversation light. And while one part of her chatted about the weather's impact on the tournament, another part worried about that look Hayden had given her when Savannah mentioned stepmothers.

Clearly he didn't expect their relationship to advance beyond the kiss-kiss, touch-touch phase. And why should he? she asked herself. In three days he would drive right out of her life, camper and boat trailer in tow... exactly what she expected and even wanted him to.

Wanted him to? Well, not exactly that, Tess realized as she nibbled a bite of crispy-fried catfish.

Since Hayden's concentration was on removing the bones from his daughter's fish, Tess stole a moment to watch him unnoticed. At once, she knew without a doubt that she did not want him to go and would actually miss him... a lot. So while their *relationship*— if she could even call it that—was strictly physical for him, it had somehow become much more to her, darn the luck.

It seemed as though her desire to protect him from the public eye was a "main" reason she hadn't given J.Q. his story after all. She couldn't be sure, of course. Hayden's tragedy was the only one she'd ever tried to report. She obviously needed more experience along that line before she made any sort of decision.

As for being anyone's stepmother.... Tess knew she'd be a fool to be insulted because Hayden seemed put off by the concept. It *was* just a tad too soon to be thinking about such a step. She almost smiled at that thought. A tad too soon? They hadn't even had a real date, for goodness' sake and not only did she not love him, she sometimes wondered if she even liked him.

"When are you going to introduce me to Fishbait?" Gracie asked, breaking into Tess's thoughts.

"How about now?" Tess replied, welcoming the opportunity to have a moment alone. Quickly she rose from the table and walked to the kitchen door, from where she beckoned to her relative.

Seconds and a brief explanation later, he accompanied her back to the table, where introductions were made.

To Tess's amazement and delight, Fishbait took one look at Gracie and then pulled up a chair to sit at their table for a few minutes, something she'd never seen him do.

"You've been at the lake since Tuesday?" Fishbait asked Gracie.

"That's right."

"How come you haven't come in here before now?"

"How do you know I haven't?" Gracie asked.

"Oh, I'd have noticed a beautiful woman like you." Fishbait looked Gracie over nearly as thoroughly as Hayden had Tess.

"Wh-why, thank you," Gracie stammered, reacting much the way Tess had. With a coy laugh, she added, "And I'd have been in sooner if I'd known the restaurant was owned by such a charmer," a reply that sounded very like flirting to Tess. Apparently it did to Hayden, too, and he appeared to be none too pleased, if somewhat shocked, by his aunt's behavior.

Fishbait had been back in the kitchen nearly a half hour before Hayden, Gracie, Savannah and Tess finished their meal. Hayden walked to the cashier to pay their bill only to be informed that the meal was on the house. Tess registered his surprise and watched him stride back into the kitchen.

Wondering what was up, she directed her gaze to the order window, through which she saw Hayden say something to Fishbait and then shake his hand. The men talked for a moment before Hayden turned and disappeared from view. A second later, he joined them in the dining room. Hayden gave no explanation, just led his harem to the door.

"How about a moonlight walk by the lake?" he asked them when they stood on the porch.

"Gracie and I can't," Savannah said. "You know we always watch *Million-Dollar Mayhum* on Thursday nights."

Hayden smiled at her mispronunciation of *mayhem*. He did, indeed, know they watched that old game show religiously. That's actually what he'd been counting on. Nonetheless, he feigned disappointment. "Oh."

"You and Tess can still go," Gracie quickly interjected. "And when you get back to the trailer, we'll have dessert." She smiled. "Coconut pie. I made it today."

Hayden groaned. "I couldn't eat another bite."

"Oh, you'll feel better after you walk," Gracie said. She took Savannah's hand, and with a smile and a wave, they left Hayden and Tess.

He turned to her. "Is a walk okay? I didn't really ask you...."

"I'd love a walk," she told him and then slipped her arm through his. Together they descended the porch steps and began a leisurely stroll toward the lake.

Illuminated by mercury vapor lights, the path was easy to traverse. They reached the shore in moments and stood in silence, listening to the water lap at the grass and rocks scattered along its edge.

Overhead, the full moon played hide-and-seek, alternately brilliant then invisible behind the storm clouds that never stopped skating across the night sky. Hayden knew he should be worried about those clouds and the rain they surely heralded. But that was the last thing on his mind at the moment.

Instead, he relished the peace of this lake that was so crowded in the light of day. Although countless tournament followers and fishing enthusiasts had begun to populate the camping areas all day, most of them seemed to be at their tents or trailers at the moment, and the few that weren't were nowhere near.

Taking advantage of that, Hayden led Tess to a wooden pier near a boat dock. They walked out over the water, and then toward the built-in benches just under the railing that lined the entire length of the structure.

"Want to sit for a minute?" he asked Tess.

"Sure."

They sat down side by side. At once, Hayden felt as awkward as some kid who'd just found out girls didn't have cooties, after all. He didn't know what to say. He didn't know what to do.

He did know he wanted to put his arm around Tess, and that's what he did, using the time-tested strategy of stretching lazily and then laying his arm along the rail supporting Tess's back.

She said nothing, just snuggled closer, a move Hayden found very encouraging. With a sigh of pleasure, he relaxed.

"Thanks for dinner," Tess said.

Hayden had to laugh. "I think that Fishbait should get all the credit."

Tess turned to look up at him. Since her face was only inches from his, the scent of her perfume filled his head. Hayden found it so intoxicating, he barely heard what she said. "What do you think of him?"

"Oh, uh, he seems like a nice enough guy."

"I think he and Gracie hit it off."

"Yeah."

"I'm glad," Tess said, reaching up to brush a lock of Hayden's hair back off his forehead. Instantly his heart slammed into his ribcage and he marveled that such a simple action could so set him on fire. "I think she probably gets lonesome for adult company."

"I suspect she does, though she won't admit it." He looked out over the lake, for the moment bathed in moonlight. "Gracie's a good woman."

"You're lucky to have her."

"You're telling me." He shook his head. "She saved my life when Sharon and I split. Saved it. I don't know how I'd have managed Savannah without her help."

"Savannah is a delightful child."

"I think so, too," Hayden said. "And I give Gracie full credit."

"Don't sell yourself short," Tess said. "I see a lot of you in your daughter."

He chuckled. "So do I ... when she's throwing a temper tantrum."

"That's not what I meant." Tess sat up straight and looked down at him. "Savannah is warm, sensitive and honest, just like her father."

"Yeah?"

"Yeah."

Rather flattered, Hayden grinned. "Why, thanks."

"Don't mention it," she said, cuddling close to him again.

Hayden liked that, and tightened his embrace to keep her just there. "Savannah really likes you, too."

"I'm glad. Though I love kids, I'm never quite sure how to act around them."

"Well, that's a problem easily solved," Hayden said. Absently he played with her hair, shimmering silvery white in the moonlight.

"Oh? How?"

"By having some of your own." Unable to resist any longer, he brushed the top of her head with his lips. "'Course, you'll have to get married before you do, and I believe you told me you had other things to accomplish first." He now gave her hair a playful tug. "As in dethroning Barbara Walters."

"I did say that, didn't I?"

"You did." Hayden frowned. "Why? Have you changed your mind about marrying?"

"No. I think I've changed my mind about becoming the next Barbara Walters."

Hayden tensed. "What do you mean?"

A long silence followed his question.

"Tess?"

"I don't mean anything," she murmured, rising to cross to the rail opposite where they sat. "Forget I said that."

He stood and followed, clasping her shoulder and turning her to face him. "Are you saying you've changed your mind about being a journalist?"

"Would you like me better if I did?" she asked, tipping her head back to look him dead in the eye.

Hayden caught his breath, struck, as always, by her beauty. "Honey," he said. "I couldn't like you much better than I already do."

"You couldn't?" She sounded disappointed, a sure indication she had misinterpreted his confession.

"No," he said. "Because if I did, I wouldn't *like* you at all. I'd—" he swallowed hard "—*love* you."

"Oh." The word fell off her lips on a whisper. She said nothing for a moment, then dropped down onto the bench. "Maybe I should reword my question." She patted the wood beside her in invitation and smiled when Hayden sat. "Would you trust me better if I weren't a reporter?"

Hayden gave her query serious consideration before replying. "No. You have my complete trust now."

Clearly as surprised by his claim as he was, Tess gave him a doubtful smile and did not reply.

At once, Hayden remembered the age-old adage that actions spoke louder than words. Why should Tess believe what he said when he'd discouraged and then ignored every personal question she had asked thus far?

"Tess, I have a story—a long, sad story—I'd like to tell you if you've got the time."

"Hey," she said. "My day will begin right here at this tournament tomorrow. If you talk all night, you'll just save me a trip home."

Hayden smiled at her nonsense and forged ahead before he changed his mind. "I first met Sharon at a fishing lodge in Missouri. She was working as a receptionist. I was the local guide. We became, uh, friendly.''

He paused for a moment as painful memories washed over him. As though sensing his distress, Tess said nothing, just slipped her arms about his waist and encouraged him with a little hug that he gladly returned.

"One thing led to another. We had an affair."

"Did you two love each other?''

''Ye—'' Hayden caught the familiar lie just in time. With something very like relief, he finally stated the painful truth. ''Actually, no. I was just too green to realize it. As for Sharon...'' He shrugged. ''She knew. And when she got pregnant, she naturally wanted to have an abortion—''

"That's not a bit natural, Hayden,'' Tess interjected.

"You know, I never thought so, either. I guess that's why I begged her to marry me and have my baby. I told her I'd do anything to make her happy. Finally she agreed."

"And did you? Make her happy, I mean?''

"I tried. So help me, I did. She wanted a house. I bought a house. She wanted a new car. I bought her a new car. It was never enough and never would be—something I didn't suspect until she asked me to give up guiding.''

"Oh, Hayden.''

"Don't worry. I didn't do it . . . at least not then. Instead I moved her and Savannah to Arkansas, close to Miller Lodge. I thought Sharon might be happier in the state where she was born and raised.''

"What happened?"

"Things definitely took a turn for the better. Unfortunately it wasn't because she'd finally settled into the role of loving wife and mother. She'd run into an old beau, Wade Waterson, who was a guest at the lodge and, believe it or not, one of my best customers. He told all his buddies to ask for me when they came to the lake. Then, when I was out fishing with them, he and Sharon would slip up to his cabin and—"

Hayden's voice cracked. Embarrassed to be so emotional over something so long past, he cleared his throat rather self-consciously before continuing.

"To make a long story short, I began to suspect, but didn't know for sure until you... well..."

"Until I showed up on your doorstep with notebook and pen in hand?"

Chapter Seven

Tess sounded regretful, he thought. Almost...
bitter. "Yeah."

"I'm so very sorry."

"It doesn't matter. If you hadn't pursued the report
of those fishermen, someone else would've and, in
fact, did. Lots of someone elses."

"I'm amazed that you've managed to keep the truth
from the press all these years."

"It wasn't easy. What saved me was the fact that no
one but Waterson, Sharon and I knew it. That, and
your keeping your promise not to squeal of course. To
this day, only one other person knows what really
happened that night. Gracie. I felt I owed her an explanation. And while I trust her implicitly, I've still
taken pains to shelter her from the press."

Silence followed that confession. Then Tess hugged
him hard.

"What's that for?" Hayden asked.

"For trusting me with your aunt. Now finish your story. I want to know what happened with Waterson and Sharon."

"When I confronted her, she admitted that the two of them had been involved, but told me that it was over."

Tess's eyes widened.

"Yeah," Hayden said. "*Over.* Apparently Waterson was quite upset about their being seen—didn't want to risk his campaign, I guess—and so broke off the relationship. Anyway, Sharon asked me to take her back, and I was naive enough to think things would be different if I did. We moved back to Missouri. I quit guiding so we could be together more. Things were okay, if not wonderful, for about four months. Then Waterson lost his election. Sharon got a phone call about three nights later and split for good. It was only after she left that I found his letters and figured out the two of them had been in contact the whole time we were in Missouri."

Tess caught her breath. "So she was lying when she said it was over?"

Hayden nodded.

"And you *still* didn't talk to reporters." He could hear that she was amazed. "You could've ruined that man's political career, you know."

"Maybe, but the price for revenge was much too high."

Tess seemed to understand that he referred to Savannah. "Where is Sharon now?"

"Hollywood...making commercials, last I heard. Apparently when Waterson really dumped her, about a year later, he made peace by setting her up in style."

"Does she ever visit Savannah?"

"No." He didn't elaborate on that.

Tess didn't ask him to. Instead, she sat up, framed his face with her hands and kissed him on the lips.

"If the hug was for trusting you, then what was that kiss for?" he asked when he could breathe again.

Tess laughed, an incredibly sexy sound he felt to the bone. "Because I couldn't wait a moment longer. I've been dying for a kiss all night, Hayden Bogart."

"That makes two of us," he said, covering her mouth with his again. One kiss turned to two, and two to three. Though quickly lost to the magic they always made, Hayden still had wits to recognize that these kisses were different than the others they had shared.

There was no frantic sampling, no hurried testing this time. They had reached a new plateau and were no longer strangers brought together by physical attraction. They were friends who cared. Friends, who could so easily be more...much more to each other....

And though he ached for her as before, he experienced none of the urgency that had ruled his actions the other times they kissed. Instead, he wanted to give and take at leisure so he could savor each precious moment they shared and build upon it. He wanted to know what pleased her and was willing to spend an eternity in the learning process, if that was what it took.

Did Tess feel the same? he wondered, even as she melted against him with a soft sigh. At once consumed with tenderness for this woman with whom he had just shared his deepest, darkest secrets, Hayden lifted Tess onto his lap and simply held her.

She rested her head in the hollow formed by his neck and shoulder and whispered, "Nice," a word that not only gave him the answer he wanted, but precisely summed up his feelings at the moment.

"Are you going to see me off tomorrow?" he murmured into her hair.

"Of course."

"Will I get a kiss for luck?"

She sat up and looked him in the eye. "In front of all those people?"

"Hmm," he teased. "That might be a bit awkward."

"I could give you one now...."

"Just one?"

Her eyes widened, as did her smile. "Just how many do you want?"

"Well, the limit is five bass. I should think at least one kiss per fish wouldn't be unreasonable."

"Okay." To Hayden's delight, Tess proceeded to kiss him...once, twice, three, four, five and then six times.

"That was one too many," Hayden said, though he hadn't minded a bit.

"Oops. Let me take it back," she replied, catching his bottom lip in her mouth and lightly sipping it.

Hayden groaned and marveled at the potency of so innocent an action. She might as well have punched him in the gut, and he knew for a certainty that if they'd been standing, he'd now be on his knees.

"Ah, Tess," he whispered. "You don't know what you're doing to this fisherman."

"So tell me."

"I'd rather show you."

"And I'd rather see than hear."

"You're tempting me," he warned.

"I'm trying to," she replied, pressing her lips to the pulse hammering so wildly in his neck.

Hayden said nothing for a moment, lost in an X-rated vision. At once something very like the old urgency consumed him, but he recognized a difference—a new depth of feeling. More than mere lust, this burning desire for Tess.

And he knew that he would never be content with a one-time fling off in the bushes somewhere. He wanted to do things right this time.

"Tess?"

"Hmm?"

"Will you think I'm crazy if I suggest that we go back and watch what's left of *Million-Dollar Mayhem?*"

She tensed, then pulled away from him. "That depends on why, I guess."

Hayden stood. Stuffing his fingertips into his pockets, he turned his back on her and stared up at the moon, now just a ghost of light, veiled as it was by clouds.

"Because I want the time to be right when I show you what you do to me. I want us to be alone with a bottle of wine, a bed, satin sheets—the works. I want a real roof over our heads, not just the night sky. I want freedom from the worry of being seen, of unwanted pregnancy, of...of—" he shrugged "—of rushing and maybe making mistakes."

Silence followed his words. Hayden could have sworn that even the lake had stilled, waiting for her reply.

Tess stood and slipped in front of him, so that he had to look at her. "You know . . . that's the sweetest thing anyone ever said to me."

"Then you're not upset?"

"No."

Anxiously he searched her face, pale in the dark. "I have a short break when the tournament is over on Sunday. I'm planning to drop Gracie and Savannah off at my parents' place for a visit. If I come back, do you think you could get off work so we could spend some time together?"

She laughed—rather dryly, he thought—then said, "Somehow I don't think that will be a problem."

Baffled by her cryptic reply, Hayden opened his mouth to question it. But at that moment Tess hugged him and banished his curiosity to parts unknown.

"What kind of pie did Gracie say she made today?" she asked, her voice muffled against his shirt.

"Coconut."

"Mmm. Coconut pie and *Million-Dollar Mayhem.* I can't think of anything more exciting."

"You can't, huh?" Heaven knows, he could.

"Well...maybe I can, but Hayden—" she tipped her head back to catch his eye "—I think you're right about our waiting. I—I just wanted you to know."

"Thanks, Tess," he said and then sent heavenward another silent thank-you not only for the treasure in his arms, but for the miracles of her understanding and his trust, something he'd once thought he'd never feel for any woman again.

* * *

Dawn on Friday found Tess at the dock, shoulder to shoulder with an amazing number of tournament officials, cameramen, fishing "widows" and "orphans" and just plain fans. She spotted a representative of the *Arkansas Daily,* as well as Bo Braden, her co-worker from the *Journal.* Tess waved when she saw him, not a bit surprised that such an enthusiast would be at the lake today.

Time and again, she scanned the crowd, looking for Hayden. She didn't see him or Gracie and Savannah yet, so made the most of her wait by soaking up the excitement, thick as the morning fog.

One by one each contestant appeared to check in and meet the observer who would go out in the boat with him to witness each and every catch. Tess watched the proceedings with avid interest and was thrilled when she finally saw Hayden and family making their way through the ever growing crowd.

Not wanting to intrude, Tess didn't draw attention to herself but stood in silence as Hayden greeted the man with whom he'd spend the next three days. That done, he hugged Savannah and placed a kiss on Gracie's cheek, then picked up his gear and started toward his boat, only to stop, turn and look straight at Tess.

Stunned that he'd located her so easily in the crush, Tess hadn't the wits to wave, much less move—even when he strode right through the crowd, took her in his arms and gave her a gigantic kiss.

"Say one for me, honey," he said, before turning on his heel and vanishing into the crowd again.

"I will," she whispered after him, very near tears as the reality of last night hit hard.

So he really did intend for them to have a relationship. A miracle, that, and one Tess had honestly doubted when she rose that morning. At once, joy filled her—joy as intense as her love for Hayden.

Love? Oh, yes. And quite caught up in it, she never doubted that he felt the same, even though he'd said nothing of the kind. At the moment, her future shone bright as the rising sun.

So, euphoric, but still a little shy, Tess wound her way through the people and joined Gracie and Savannah.

"Hi," she said.

"Hi, yourself," Gracie replied, clearly delighted to see her. Savannah, too, looked rather pleased, and her twinkling eyes told Tess that she'd most likely seen Hayden's bold kiss. The child said nothing, though, and the three of them turned their attention back to the tournament just in time to see the last contestant board his boat.

Side by side, the contestants waited at the lake's edge until, promptly at 6:00 a.m., Tess heard the crack of a starter's gun. Immediately twenty-five motors roared to life and, en masse, the boats sped out across the lake to this or that contestant's favorite fishing hole.

Tess had never seen or heard anything quite like it, and laughed aloud with the exhilaration of the moment. What fun! And to think that she would be part of it again, not only that weekend, but for many weekends to come.

"Well, that's that," Gracie commented from nearby. "Now we play a waiting game." She turned to Tess. "Would you like to come in and have breakfast with us?"

"I can't," Tess said with genuine regret. Now that she and Hayden were a sure thing, she was ready—no, eager—to begin building a relationship with his family. "I have to go to work. I will be back this afternoon, though. I thought I might interview some of the contestants' wives . . . for my next report."

"I know most of them," Gracie said. "I could introduce you."

"Oh, would you?" Tess smiled. "Thanks a bunch." She turned to Savannah. "What are you going to do today?"

"Me and Cindy Lawrence are going to play."

"Cindy . . . ?" Tess looked to Gracie for explanation.

"Daughter of one of the fishermen," the woman said. "They arrived at the lake late last night, right after you left, actually."

"You're all very close aren't you?" Tess said.

Gracie laughed. "I guess we are. Heaven knows I see more of most of them than I do my own kin."

At once Tess wanted to be a part of this "family" of fishermen and their wives who traveled the tournament trail. And it was with reluctance that she took her leave moments later and went home to dress for a job that had once been her everything, but now played second fiddle to love.

Though fully anticipating a run-in with J.Q., Tess didn't even see him all day. It was almost as though he avoided her. Baffled but relieved, she made the most of the situation and worked quietly at her desk until lunchtime.

Her thoughts often drifted from the task at hand—writing up weddings for Sunday's bridal section—to the man she loved. How was he doing? she couldn't help but wonder as she glanced out the window time and again to check the weather.

Though the sky had changed from clear to overcast, no rain fell. Tess smiled to herself, pleased that Hayden would not have the added stress of trying to stay dry.

After finishing up the weddings, Tess turned her attention to the fact sheets provided by the local funeral home. Though she didn't always know the citizens she profiled in the obituaries, she always felt for them and for those loved ones left behind.

Today was no exception, and gloom settled over Tess like a blanket as she read the facts regarding one particular woman.

Age: sixty. *So young.* Occupation: housewife. *Lucky lady.*

Lucky lady? A woman who'd done nothing more than marry, have babies, clean and cook? Why, she'd left no mark in the world. No mark.

Except a successful husband. And three children, one a lawyer, one a soldier and one a young mother with children of her own. Without a doubt, this dead woman's work meant more in the scheme of things than any interview with some celebrity—Tess's career goal for the past three years.

As her vision filled with tears of sympathy for the family of this woman, Tess suddenly remembered another dream she'd once had—a dream even older than her recently resurrected one to be a teacher.

She closed her eyes, picturing herself at Savannah's age, dragging around a doll named Tammy, changing its diapers, "feeding" it a bottle. She'd told everyone who asked that she wanted to be a "mommy" when she grew up.

When had she changed her mind—chosen a career over marriage?

More important, what would happen if she now did an about-face... walked right out of this office, away from the stress of this job she *didn't* love and into the arms of the man she *did?*

Tess didn't know and pondered the question until eleven-thirty, at which time she laughed aloud at her foolish thoughts. Hayden had done nothing more than promise to come back and see her after he took Gracie and Savannah to Missouri. He hadn't said he loved her. He certainly hadn't proposed.

She would be crazy to read something everlasting into what was most likely only momentary, mutual desire. Still... it was hard to push her "forever after" thoughts aside.

When she finally closed up shop, anxious to see her first real report in print, Tess checked the status of that evening's edition. As expected, it wasn't out yet, and promising herself she would buy one out of the paper box at the Catch-N-Cook, Tess walked to her car and headed for the lake.

She parked near Hayden's camper, knocked on his door and was immediately greeted by Savannah and another child, most likely Cindy. The two girls beckoned Tess inside, where Savannah made introductions.

"This is my daddy's girlfriend," she announced. "I've seen them kiss."

Cindy thought about that for a moment. "My daddy doesn't have a girlfriend."

Savannah rolled her eyes. "Of course not, silly. Your daddy has a wife. She used to be his girlfriend, though. That's how these things work."

"I don't remember it," Cindy said.

"You weren't born," Savannah told her. She looked at Tess and sighed. "She just doesn't get it."

"I do, too!" Cindy retorted so loudly that Tess winced.

"Do not."

"Do, too."

They squared off, clearly prepared to do battle. At a loss, Tess stepped forward to break them apart just as Gracie glided into the room. "Girls, girls. That's enough of that." She started when she saw Tess and smiled. "Why, hello, dear. I didn't hear you come in. How was your morning?"

"Fine," Tess told her. "How about yours?"

Gracie hesitated. "Um, busier than expected. I didn't get a thing done." She glanced at the clock. "Cindy, I believe it's time for me to walk you home. Would you like to go along, Tess? Cindy's mother, Carla, has been traveling the tournament circuit for three years. She'd be a good resource person for your article."

"Do you think she'd mind?" Tess asked.

"She'd love it," Gracie replied, then led the way to the door. She said little else on the walk through the campsite or during Tess's subsequent visit with Carla and two other wives. Tess noted the uncharacteristic reticence and wondered if Gracie had another headache.

It wasn't until the three of them walked back to the camper that she had a chance to ask her.

"You're awfully quiet. Do you have another headache?"

"No."

"Is something else wrong?"

"N-no." But Gracie wouldn't meet her gaze.

And since she wouldn't, Tess really began to worry. "You're not upset about Hayden's kissing me this morning are you? I couldn't bear it if—"

"Oh, no." Gracie managed a wan smile. "I'm so very glad that you two...well...that Hayden has finally shown an interest in someone. I'm especially glad it's you." She sighed and glanced quickly at Savannah, who'd run ahead several paces. "May I confide in you?"

"Of course," Tess replied, sincerely concerned now.

"Today I..." Gracie paused, then shrugged and laughed lightly. "On second thought, never mind."

"But—"

"*Never mind.* Now why don't we go inside and have another piece of coconut pie before we go down to the dock and wait for the guys?"

"All right," Tess said, shelving her disappointment that Gracie hadn't shared her problem, whatever it was. There would be other times, other problems, she told herself. And she was foolish to be hurt because Hayden's aunt wasn't ready to confide in someone she'd known a grand total of four—could it really be only *four?*—days.

Chapter Eight

After eating the pie, Gracie, Savannah and Tess walked to the dock, where a crowd had begun to gather. Tess waved to her new friends, also waiting for their men, and struck up a conversation, deliberately including Gracie in hopes of shaking her out of her gloom. Savannah and Cindy, not a bit interested in the proceedings, began to play with some other children nearby.

The minutes ticked away. The sky changed from blue to coral, heralding dusk. One by one the fishermen returned to the dock. By check-in time that evening, the area bustled with activity and the air crackled with excitement.

Of one accord, the family and fans gravitated to the lighted wooden platform where the ABFA president, who served as master of ceremonies, stood ready to interview the contestants and weigh in their day's catch.

Tess noted the care with which scores were tallied and posted. There was no doubting the fairness of the tournament. Observers had witnessed every catch. Fans now witnessed every weigh in.

Since Hayden's catch was the fifteenth to be registered, Tess's stomach knotted with anticipation before he stepped up on the platform, plastic bag of fish in hand and dripping clear lake water.

She crossed her fingers—as though that childish action would really make a difference—and said yet another prayer that Hayden would do well today. She then tried to read his expression for a clue as to whether or not he had. It wasn't easy. His friendly smile and joking conversation with the master of ceremonies gave nothing away.

Finally, the oversize digital scale lighted to display the weight of the five bass Hayden had placed in the weigh basket. Tess noted the figures and sagged with disappointment. At the moment, Hayden placed eighth of fifteen, and ten more fishermen still waited in the wings, ready to weigh their trophies.

Beside her, Gracie sighed. They exchanged a rueful glance, then moved together toward Hayden's boat, where he now waited, clearly discouraged, though he greeted them both with a smile.

"Nothing went right today," he said, kissing his aunt on the cheek, then reaching out for Savannah, who'd run up to join them. He hefted his daughter up into his arms and hugged her. "I broke my favorite rod. Hung up every darn time I cast, and lost a fish that would've weighed three, maybe four pounds."

"Don't be sad," Savannah said, patting his sunburned cheek. "I bet you'll do better tomorrow."

"I hope so." He set his daughter on her feet, then quickly pulled Tess into his arms. His tight hug stole her breath, as did the kiss he added to it.

"They're kissing *again*," Savannah whispered rather loudly to Gracie with visible awe. "Does that mean Tess is going to sleep with him?"

"Savannah!" Gracie gasped, her face flushing crimson.

Clearly baffled by her baby-sitter's shock, Savannah looked from one to the other of the three adults now staring at her. "But that's what they do on *Nassau Nights*."

Hayden let a very embarrassed Tess slip free of his embrace, then glared at his aunt. "I thought you told me you'd quit watching those damn soaps."

Gracie gave him a sheepish smile. "All but that one. I didn't think she was old enough to know what was going on."

"Well, it appears you were wrong," Hayden said.

An awkward quiet followed. Uncomfortable with it, Tess hastily changed the subject to keep the peace. "The weathermen are predicting a ninety percent chance of rain tomorrow."

"I heard," he murmured, running his fingers through his windblown hair. "It doesn't look good, Tess."

"What are you talking about?" she retorted. "This is only the first day of the tournament, and you know every drop of water in this lake. You're going to do fine."

"Of course you are," Gracie chimed in. "Now why don't you get cleaned up, and I'll fix you a bite to eat." She turned to Tess. "If I know him, he didn't have anything but water all day. He gets that nervous in these tournaments."

"Do you really?" Tess asked, as always fascinated by everything about him.

Hayden shrugged. "Yeah, but I usually make up for it when I get home, and tonight will be no exception. We've been invited to a cookout at Randy Quick's over in area D. He's a fellow contestant and an old friend," Hayden added for Tess's benefit.

"Can Tess come, too?" Savannah asked, jumping up and down with excitement.

"I'm counting on it." Those four words made Tess's heart sing.

It sang even louder a short time later when Hayden introduced her to his fishing buddies as his girlfriend. How she basked in his attention. How she loved the way he kept his arm hooked so possessively around her waist.

Everyone made her feel welcome, and as the night progressed and they all shared the fun of roasted hot dogs and the warmth of a camp fire, Tess began to feel as though she'd known these good folks forever and was truly one of them.

At eight o'clock, Gracie announced that she was exhausted. Once more concerned for her, Tess volunteered to walk her back to the camper. Her offer was waved away, however, and after gathering up an equally exhausted Savannah, Gracie left them.

Barely thirty minutes later, the party broke up. Tess wasn't surprised since most everyone would have to be up before dawn the next morning. For that reason, she refused Hayden's invitation to come inside the camper by asking him to accompany her to the Catch-N-Cook so she could buy the Friday edition of the *Jenner Springs Journal*.

They walked together the short distance, hand in hand, each relishing the closeness and the quiet. Tess put some quarters in the box and extracted two newspapers from it, one of which she gave to Hayden.

She then ignored the lure of the lake and another moonlight stroll by purposefully leading him back to his family.

"'Night, Hayden," she said to him when they reached his door.

"You're not going to sleep with me?" he asked, pulling her into his arms. "Savannah will be awfully disappointed."

"She'll get over it," Tess said. She ducked the kiss he tried to give her. In her current frame of mind, kisses would never be enough, and the man needed his strength for the next day's fishing competition.

"I'll see you tomorrow?"

"Of course, and the day after, and for as many days as you want to see me."

He tensed. "You mean that?"

"I mean it." Dead silence followed her candid admission—silence so long that she began to wonder if she had spoken out of turn, imagined love where there was none. Instantly she tried to pull free. But he wouldn't let her this time.

"No—" She heard him swallow. "It's just that I never thought I'd find someone like you. I figured happy endings only happened in those fairy tales that Gracie reads to Savannah."

"So did I, but we were wrong."

"I—I think I love you, Tess."

She caught her breath at his sweet, stammered confession. "And I think I love you."

He gave her a shaky smile. "We need to talk."

"And we will ... after the tournament, when I can have your full attention."

"Honey, you've got it now," he said, tracing her curves with his hands, pressing his lips to hers again. Unable to resist any longer, Tess gave in to his fevered kiss, then paid for her folly when a wave of new desire washed over her.

"That's not what I meant, and you know it," she exclaimed, playfully slapping his brazen, magical hands away. "I don't want the uncertainty of this competition hanging over our heads."

"But, Tess—"

"Please."

He searched her face, then nodded and stepped back with obvious reluctance. "I suppose you're right. I had a heck of a time concentrating today as it was."

"I'm not surprised. Now you go inside and go to bed. You look exhausted."

"I do, huh?" He chuckled, a marvelously sexy sound that shook her resolve to leave. "Well, exhausted is not at all the word I would use to describe what I'm feeling right now."

"Which would you use?" she asked in spite of her better judgment.

"Excited."

Her heart thumped once, then went berserk. "What did you say?"

"Excited ... as in *verrry* stimulated. Do you know what I mean by that?"

"Yes." The word came out a squeak.

"Sure? 'Cause if you're not, I'll be glad to demonstrate. We'll spread a blanket off in the bushes somewhere, cuddle up, kiss a bit. I can almost guarantee that before the night is old you'll know exactly what I mean by 'excited'—"

Tess could almost guarantee it, too, and put a hand to his lips to shush his vivid plans. "I thought you said you wanted us to have a roof over our heads when we, uh . . . you know."

"I said that?" He sounded quite incredulous.

Taking advantage of his discomfiture, Tess stepped back a pace. "You did, and I agreed with you. So good night, Hayden."

"Sure you won't change your mind?"

"Sure." She said it with genuine regret.

"Then good night," he said, clearly as remorseful. "Sleep tight."

"And don't let the *bad* bugs bite?"

"The *what?*"

"Never mind. Now don't forget to read my article. And while you're at it, you might want to read the rest of the newspaper. For a small-town publication, we're not half bad."

"I'll do that," he promised.

Not thirty minutes after Tess drove off in her car, Hayden stepped into a stinging cold shower. While the water sizzled against his overheated body, he reviewed the amazing conversation he'd just had with Tess.

She loved him. Well, *thought* she did, anyway. He grinned at the qualification—one he'd used himself—and vowed that soon she would know for sure, just as he really did now.

How good it felt to be wholehearted again. How good to trust.

He'd always heard that time could heal any hurt. Perhaps that was true, but Hayden believed more than time had produced his miraculous recovery.

He gave credit to Tess, a woman like no other. The woman he loved.

After drying off and dressing in sweats, Hayden made his way to the kitchen. A quick glance toward Savannah's bunk revealed that she slept soundly, a sure sign that she had played hard all day. Gracie, too, slept...or so he assumed. The door to her bedroom was shut and no light shone from underneath it.

Humming softly, he made himself a ham sandwich, then poured a glass of milk and sat at the table to eat. There he spied the newspaper Tess had given him, and smiling as he recalled her excitement, he reached for it.

Taking her advice to read the whole thing, he scanned the bold black headlines on the front page. He saw a report about the latest labor strike, a report about the president's impending trip abroad and a report about... Wade Waterson, gubernatorial candidate, *ladies' man.*

Hayden tensed when he read those words—tensed and zoomed in on the story, written by someone named Bo Braden. With growing outrage, he read the "little known" facts of a "torrid love affair" between the "suave" politician and one, Sharon Bogart, ex-wife of Hayden Bogart, a former guide at Miller Lodge, who just happened to be in town fishing in the ABFA tournament.

Heart pounding, cheeks aflame, Hayden read truths revealed by a "source close to Hayden Bogart"—

among them the details of Sharon's before-the-wedding pregnancy and the name of the daughter she never called or visited.

And, as if that weren't enough, the writer of the article had run what looked to be a very recent photograph of Sharon, hanging on the arm of a well-known movie producer, who had a squeaky-clean reputation.

Hayden barely registered the photo, so shocked was he by the exposé. The next instant, his shock turned to gut-twisting confusion and that confusion to outright rage as the truth hit home.

Tess had betrayed him.

Betrayed him.

The woman he loved. The woman he trusted.

Why? he agonized, at once confused again. Why would she do such a thing?

That the "source" *was* Tess, he had no doubt. No one else who knew the truth stood to gain anything from the exposé—certainly not Wade, who had his political career to think of, or Sharon, now linked romantically to a man of solid moral fiber. As for Gracie, he didn't give that possibility a second thought.

It could only be Tess, who struggled to follow in her famous father's footsteps. Livid at her for using him—and at himself for letting her—Hayden spat out an expletive and slammed the newspaper down on the table. He snatched up his truck keys and stalked to the door, fully intending to drive to Tess's and confront her with her treachery.

Halfway to his vehicle, he stopped short and cursed again. How could he confront Tess when he didn't even know where she lived? Hell, he didn't even know her phone number.

And that wasn't all.... With a start, Hayden realized just how little he really knew about this woman who'd so easily stolen his heart. Besides the fact that her father was a famous reporter and that she had two brothers, Hayden had learned next to nothing about Tess's life, past and present. That was only natural, of course. Tess had been conducting an interview most of the time they were together. Nonetheless, Hayden wished he'd slipped in a few more questions of his own.

Fuming, fearful of waking his sleeping family, he pivoted sharply and strode to the lake, where he passed the next half hour alternately cursing and throwing rocks into the water. Neither relieved his agony, or soothed his rage.

What a fool he'd been to trust Tess. How neatly he'd fallen prey to her innocent smile, her glib promises, her beautiful body—a body she'd offered him more than once.

He laughed bitterly when he recalled his noble attempts to do right by her and imagined how relieved she must have been that she hadn't had to sleep with the fat man to get the scoop.

Disgusted, Hayden walked out on the pier and sat where he and Tess had sat another time. Unbidden, memories of their sweet idyll came to him. He could almost taste her kiss, smell her perfume.... How could she have fooled him so utterly? he wondered, even as he acknowledged that it must not be that hard to do. He'd swallowed Sharon's lies for years...hook, line and sinker.

Not a bit amused by the metaphor, which most likely resulted from too many hours with a fishing rod, Hayden buried his face in his hands. He told himself he was well rid of her. But his eyes stung with hot tears of regret.

Roaring his disgust, Hayden lunged to his feet and stomped back down the pier. With long strides he covered the short distance to his camper and flung open the door.

A squeal of surprise greeted his dramatic entry. Instantly contrite, Hayden apologized to the dear woman who had uttered it.

Gracie said nothing in reply, just in the eating booth, staring at the newspaper she held in her hand. Hayden noted her white-knuckled clench and sat across from her in the booth.

"Oh, Hayden, I'm so sorry," she murmured, eyes brimming.

"Don't apologize for her."

"Her...?" Gracie frowned. Then her eyes widened. "You mean you think..."

Belatedly, Hayden realized that his aunt hadn't figured out who "the source" was. "Tess talked."

"No."

"Yes." Gently he took the newspaper and laid it on the table, then covered his aunt's hands with his and stroked them. "It had to be her." He shook his head with the disbelief he still felt himself. "Had to be. What an actress. You should've seen her tonight, making such a big deal out of buying this stupid paper and giving it to me to read."

Lost in the painful memory, Hayden didn't notice Gracie's silence or her look of horror.

"Helluva way to say goodbye, wasn't it? But maybe she did me a favor taking the coward's way out. God knows I might have made a fool of myself and begged if I hadn't known what she really is..." At once a wave of self-pity washed over Hayden. His voice trailed to silence, and with difficulty he swallowed the lump in his throat.

Gracie still said nothing, but he saw one tear and then another splash onto the table. Immediately Hayden pushed his own hurt aside.

"Don't cry," he blurted, slipping around the table to lay an arm awkwardly across Gracie's shoulders. His words, instead of soothing his aunt, made her cry harder—racking sobs that almost frightened him with their intensity.

"Hush now," he soothed rather awkwardly as he patted her shoulder. "We're not hurt. Not a bit. We'll forget all about her and we'll survive this just like we've survived everything else."

His aunt said nothing, just pulled free with a strangled cry and dashed down the hall, her old chenille robe billowing out behind her. A second later, Hayden heard the door shut.

Fury anew consumed him. Fists clenched, he vowed that Tess would pay for the hurt she'd inflicted on his innocent family.

As for what she'd done to him, he deserved it—deserved it for being a damn fool, for lowering his guard, for falling in love with her.

Arms laden with the milk, bread, lunch meat and paper plates that were such a necessity these days, Tess backed up against her door and pushed it open. Once in her kitchen, she made short work of putting away her purchases, then snatched up the *Journal* and headed right to the living room, where she plopped down in her chair.

Ignoring her own advice to read the whole newspaper, Tess flipped to the sports section and her article without so much as a glance at the front page.

Local Fishing Tournament Raises Controversy announced the bold black print on page fifteen. Under that headline, in smaller print, she read the words *by Tess Fremont,* and laughed with delight.

Her first story.

And, most likely, her last... unless a miracle occurred and J.Q. let her go ahead and do the follow-ups she had originally planned. Tess doubted that and so analyzed her feelings at that moment. She registered excitement and pleasure. She registered pride.

But nowhere, even in her heart of hearts, did she find regret that she might never report for the *Journal* again. Tess smiled, knowing she owed her peace of mind to Hayden, who loved her not because she was a reporter, but in spite of it.

Quickly she read the article, which J.Q. had printed with amazingly little editing. Sighing her satisfaction, Tess then closed the paper. She walked through the kitchen, tossed the newspaper onto the table, then headed for the bedroom and the big ol' bed in which she would not "sleep tight" until the man she loved shared it with her.

The next morning, Tess rose—with the help of her alarm clock—before the sun came up. She dressed quickly, then went into the kitchen to toast an English muffin for her breakfast.

With a quick glance at the clock, Tess snatched up her purse and dashed out the door headed to Miller

Lake. Not only could she not wait another minute to hear what Hayden thought of her story, she was determined to get there in time to walk with him and his family from the camper to the dock.

The sky seemed unusually dark for the hour when Tess braked her car just outside Hayden's camper a few minutes later. She killed the engine, then climbed out of her vehicle and glanced heavenward, noting the ever-present storm clouds. A quick sniff confirmed the likelihood that the rain that had fallen off and on all night would soon fall again.

Poor Hayden, she thought, her gaze now on his lighted camper. In mere moments he would be heading toward the dock where she could already see a crowd gathering. Undoubtedly, he would spend his day battling the elements.

Carefully Tess made her way over a carpet of sodden pine needles. Just as she reached the camper, the inside light flicked off and the door flew open. A second later, Hayden stepped outside alone. He stopped short when he saw her and with a quick glance back over his shoulder, pulled the door firmly shut behind him.

"What in the hell are you doing here?" he demanded much to her astonishment, striding over to grasp her upper arm and as good as drag her back to her car.

"Why, I—I came to see you off," she stammered, shocked by his scowl and his crushing grip.

"You came to—?" With a growl of pure rage, Hayden grabbed her other arm and pulled her up close. "Do you have any idea what you've done to my family? Any idea at all?"

"What are you talking about?" she blurted, clinging to him to keep on her feet.

Hayden released her so abruptly, she stumbled back against her car. He drew in a shaky breath, clearly struggling for control, then slowly exhaled. "I don't know what game you're playing, but I do know this. If you ever come near my aunt or child again, you'll have me to reckon with. Understand?"

Tess, trying to unravel the mystery of his behavior, couldn't have answered if she'd tried.

"Understand?" he repeated, stepping near again, burning holes right through her with the fire in his eyes.

"Y-yes," she managed to gasp, backing away from him. "I mean no. No, I don't understand."

He stared at her for a moment, clearly astonished by her reply, then laughed—a scary sound that sent shivers dancing up Tess's spine.

"Lady, you deserve an Oscar for this performance," he spat at her. "It's even better than last night's."

That said, he whirled and stalked away, headed through sprinkling rain to the mist-enshrouded lake.

Chapter Nine

Though sorely tempted to follow him and demand some answers, Tess didn't dare. Hayden had made it quite clear that he didn't want her around. She had too much pride to chase after him.

Fighting tears, Tess glanced uncertainly toward the camper. Obviously Gracie and Savannah were not going to see Hayden off today, probably due to the bad weather. In spite of Hayden's warning to stay clear of the two of them, she desperately wanted to talk to his aunt, who probably had the answers she needed.

But in the end, Tess never made a move in that direction. Though she wasn't a bit afraid of Hayden, who'd already proved he couldn't even hurt a fish, she harbored a very real fear that Gracie and Savannah might be as angry at her, too. Definitely not up to another mystifying rejection at the moment, Tess came to a quick decision and whirled to get into her car.

Coffee, that's what she needed. Strong. Black. The kind for which Fishbait was famous. The kind that could clear the cobwebs of confusion from her brain.

Her mind on the pot undoubtedly brewing in her relative's kitchen, Tess skirted the dock traffic and drove the short distance to the Catch-N-Cook. She would drink a cup, maybe two of the magical stuff, and, only when fully functional again, would try to figure out what had just happened.

By the time Tess reached the restaurant, steady rain swept her windshield. Ducking against the downpour, which felt downright icy to her flushed face, Tess dashed onto the covered porch. She stood there a moment to catch her breath, then stepped toward the door, only to halt abruptly when her gaze fell on the nearby newspaper box, wherein lay one last issue of last night's *Journal*.

Its bold headline leapt right out at her this morning, and with a strangled gasp, Tess dropped to her knees and read the byline through the clear plastic front of the box. Heart pounding like crazy, she then scanned the article.

''Oh, no,'' she breathed when she reached the words *source close to Hayden Bogart*.

Surely he didn't think…. But of course he did. Why else would he attack this morning?

Obviously Hayden believed *she* was the ''source'' who'd talked.

Wounded to the heart by that realization, Tess lost her battle for control and burst into tears that surely rivaled the summer squall. Though blinded by them, she somehow found the way back to her car, in which she sat and sobbed in earnest for a full minute before she regained some measure of calm.

Her first impulse was to drive straight away from this hurtful man who could vow love in one breath and threaten her in the next. Following through on that impulse, Tess actually fumbled through her pocket for the key and even stuck it in the ignition.

But instead of turning it, she just sat there, in spite of everything unable to exit Hayden's life... at least until she cleared her name.

Cleared her name?

"Clear my name," Tess reaffirmed aloud, as though saying those three words might make them true. She knew better, of course, and disgusted by her apparent addiction to Hayden, fought new tears.

How quickly he'd jumped to conclusions. How quickly. So much for all his words of love. Wouldn't most men in love have assumed she was innocent or at least given her a chance to defend herself?

Tess thought so.

But Hayden wasn't most men. He was special—a man who'd been to hell and back, a man now haunted by the memory. How he must have hurt when he read that awful story... probably as much as she hurt now. And Tess's heart went out to him in spite of her belief that he should have trusted in her.

So what now? she wondered, staring through the rainwashed windshield toward the crowd standing back at the dock, most of them huddled under umbrellas or whatever other shelter they could find.

Tess soon came to realize that she had two choices. She could put her pride in her pocket and leave the only man she'd ever loved, or she could toss that pride in the trash and fight for him. It was as simple as that.

And equally simple was her decision. Since Tess couldn't imagine life without Hayden, she knew she had to "fight," knew she had to tell him the truth: someone else had talked.

But what someone else? Tess wondered, her tears now reduced to an occasional sniffle.

Since no one but Bo Braden knew the answer to that question, Tess made another simple decision and crawled out of her car again. She scurried back up on the porch then entered the restaurant, heading straight for the pay phone, tucked away in a corner.

There, Tess grabbed up the phone book. A second later, she dialed the reporter's number. A woman answered it first ring and told Tess that Bo was at Miller Lake, information that did not surprise Tess now that she thought about it.

After mumbling her thanks, Tess hung up the phone and glanced at her watch. She was amazed to discover that five minutes still remained before the fishermen left the dock . . . if they ever did.

Tess, herself, could not imagine that anyone could actually fish in this rain, even though Hayden had talked about several tournaments held in inclement weather. It seemed the fishermen didn't mind, if there was no lightning or wind, of course.

Though not one of those hardy sportsmen, she headed back outside and ran across the parking lot the few yards to the dock, where an amazing number of people stood, soaked to the skin, waiting for the crack of the starting pistol.

Just as Tess neared the edge of the crowd, she heard that crack and the instantaneous, earthshaking roar of twenty-five outboard motors.

"They're out of their minds," she mumbled, watching the shoreline empty of boats and fishermen. Hunching her shoulders against the wet, Tess scanned the crowd for Bo. She didn't see him, but saw his car parked in the lot and so made her way in that direction. Surely he wouldn't hang around in this kind of weather.

As expected, the crowd dispersed shortly after—no picnics today. Many got into their cars and left. Others headed toward the Catch-N-Cook, no doubt for the hot coffee she had yet to drink. Tess, now shivering next to Bo's car, sighed her relief when the rain slacked off some, and again when she finally saw the red-haired reporter walking toward his vehicle about five minutes later.

"Why, hello, Tess." He gave her his usual cocky grin. "Nice weather, huh?"

"Got a minute?" Tess asked, in no mood for jokes or chitchat. "I'd like to talk to you."

Bo shrugged. "Why not? We're both already soaked."

"Where did you get your story?" Tess asked without further ado.

"Which one? I've done so many. . . ."

Tess barely held her temper in check. "The Waterson scoop, Bo. Who talked?"

"Tsk, tsk," he shot back. "You know as well as I do that a good reporter never reveals his sources. Or maybe you *don't* know it."

"What's that supposed to mean?" Tess asked, surprised by the taunt and the sudden hostility of his tone.

"That you probably aren't even aware there *are* rules to good reporting."

"Don't be ridiculous. I've been with the *Journal* longer than you have."

He laughed at that. "Only because your old man and J.Q. are buddies. If I'd pulled some of the stunts you've pulled, I'd have been out on my ear long ago."

Tess caught her breath at the insult. "That isn't true. J.Q. loves my work."

"You call writing up obituaries from a funeral parlor fact sheet 'work'? A ninth-grader could do what you do, Tess. As for J.Q. loving it—" Bo laughed again. "As long as you're not playing reporter, he'll love anything you do. But when he needs a real pro— like for the Waterson story—he talks to me."

Tess tensed. "When did he do that?"

"Right after our staff meeting on Wednesday. It was short notice, but, as usual, I came through."

So J.Q. had never believed for a moment she would be able to get the exposé. No wonder he hadn't said anything about her failure to do so. He'd expected it. That hurt...and made her wonder if Bo was right, and she'd only kept her job all these years because of her dad.

At once, shame brought heat to her cheeks. Swallowing back the lump of humiliation now threatening her breathing, Tess somehow managed a sardonic smile.

"You came through all right. I'm just sorry that innocent people will have to pay the price for your devotion to duty."

"Wade Waterson is no innocent," Bo replied, hooking a thumb through the belt loops of his soaked jeans, leaning back against his shiny red sportster.

"What about Hayden's aunt and his daughter? What about the rest of his family? They're certainly not to blame for Waterson's sins."

"That kid of his can't be more than what...? Three, four years old? Too young to know what's going on, or to care. As for that aunt of his... I think she's a few bricks short of a full load. She'll never notice, either." He suddenly tensed, as though he'd let something slip, and then straightened to reach for the door handle. "But I don't have to defend myself to you. I was told to get a story, and I got it."

"You certainly did," Tess dryly agreed, stepping back to let him open the door. Whether or not Bo knew it—and she thought perhaps he did—he'd just given away his "source": Gracie. Very distressed by that unexpected news, it was all Tess could do to act normal. "And I'm sure J.Q. is very proud of you. I just hope you can sleep nights."

He snorted at that and slipped behind the wheel. "Hey, my conscience is clean," he said, then shut the door.

"Yours, maybe," Tess murmured to herself, as the engine roared to life and the car sped away. "But I think I know someone whose isn't." She watched until the vehicle disappeared from view, then looked thoughtfully toward the camper, just visible through the pine thicket.

Clearly, it was time for that talk with Gracie, time to get those answers. But what if the answers confirmed her worst fears? Tess couldn't help but wonder.

Wouldn't getting them result in a new dilemma—namely whether or not to tell Hayden the truth?

Tess believed it would. She knew how much Hayden loved his aunt—far more than he might love Tess—and knew how much Gracie's betrayal would hurt him—again, far more than Tess's. Nonetheless, she headed toward the camper. She had to know if Gracie talked to Bo. Had to.

Halfway there, she recognized the folly of her determination and veered sharply to the left, destination: her car. There would be time to confront Gracie later that morning, she realized, when she could be more certain that the woman was awake and had consumed at least one cup of morning coffee.

At the moment, Tess had other unanswered—and, now that she thought about it, *unasked*—questions every bit as pressing, questions raised by Bo's comments moments ago.

Had her boss kept her employed because she'd done a good job these three years? Or was Bo right about the influence of an old friendship with her dad?

Only J. Q. Southerland knew the answers. And pride propelled Tess to the *Jenner Springs Journal* where he could always be found early on a Saturday—or any other—morning.

Clear across the vast lake, Hayden slowed his engine and steered the boat toward one of his favorite fishing spots—one where he'd often caught bass on other rainy days. A second later, he killed the engine and coasted in the remaining distance.

With a nod to the tournament observer who shared his boat, Hayden straightened his waterproof poncho and his cap, then reached for one of his rods. He checked his chartreuse-colored lure, one guaranteed to tempt a fish even on a gloomy day like this, and made his cast.

As Hayden began to reel in his line—an automatic motion resulting from years of practice—his thoughts turned to Tess and her baffling behavior that morning.

Try as he might, he could not understand why she would show up at his door as though innocent as a lamb. Surely, *surely* she realized what she'd done by spilling her guts to Bo Whatsisname, that reporter. Hayden sure as hell knew what *he'd* done by spilling his to her.

Had she thought he might not guess who'd talked? Hayden didn't see how she could. After spending so much time with him, she certainly realized he was no fool.

Or did she? Hayden winced, in retrospect deciding he'd pretty much acted the idiot all week...at least over her.

And undoubtedly recognizing his weakness in the head, Tess had felt confident to use the information he'd given her to get ahead in her career, even if it ruined him.

Ruined *him?* Hayden frowned. Well, not exactly that. The only man ruined was Wade Waterson, who deserved a little bad press to Hayden's way of thinking. As for the *woman* who'd been ruined, Hayden was just vengeful enough not to care about her.

Sharon thrived on attention. And though this sort of notoriety might not do wonders for her acting career or her relationship with her current beau, Hayden had no doubt she would survive and probably benefit from it in some way.

She usually did.

So why did Tess's betrayal bother him so much if it couldn't ruin him? Hayden wondered. Was it because of the resulting possibility of being hounded by reporters again?

Hayden seriously considered that...and decided not.

He'd had years of dealing with reporters. He knew how to handle them now.

Was it, then, the embarrassment of being revealed as Sharon's cuckold? Hayden next mused as he went through the motions of casting, reeling, recasting and rereeling. He thought about that a moment, trying on such a label for size. He felt no shame for trusting Sharon or for trying so hard to save his marriage by giving her another chance even after he knew the truth about her affair. If others thought him crazy, that was their problem. He didn't care.

So why did Tess's betrayal hurt so much? he asked himself yet again. The word *betrayal* echoed loudly in his head and at once Hayden suspected the reason for his misery—a reason so obvious he almost laughed.

"Man, oh, man," he immediately murmured, zeroing in on that suspicion. But even as Hayden formulated it into a rational possibility, a strong gust of wind came from nowhere and lifted the hem of his heavy poncho. Momentarily distracted from his worries, he turned and glanced sharply back at his companion, whose gaze was not on his fishing rod but on the swirling heavens.

Hayden stopped reeling and glanced skyward himself. He frowned at what he saw there: rolling gray-green clouds that could very well produce big winds and hail.

He suddenly wondered if the tournament should have been canceled, at least for that day. But no. They'd taken a vote. Besides, everyone had fished in the rain before, most of them in a tournament situation.

And there was no wind . . . well, there hadn't been at six o'clock, starting time. Now there were gusts aplenty.

"We'd best keep an eye on those clouds," the observer said.

"Just what I was thinking," Hayden murmured even as the boat dipped sharply in the crest of a wave. A quick inspection of the lake revealed other waves, some of them white caps.

A vague, very uncharacteristic feeling of unease came over Hayden. He glanced toward his companion, a local fisherman who'd won some kind of radio contest for the privilege of being an observer in today's competition.

Though Hayden stood to lose a whole day's fishing if they returned to the dock, he seriously considered that possibility. He had the welfare of his family to think about, as did this young observer.

He also had something else: a burning need to see Tess again, to ask one very important question that had nothing to do with the *Jenner Springs Journal*. And if she gave him the right answer, well, they had a lot to talk about. . . .

A hell of a lot.

* * *

Tess's watch said eight-thirty when she parked her car next to Hayden's camper again. She sat for a moment without moving, a half smile of satisfaction on her face even though she'd just quit her job.

Well, not *quit*, exactly. Tess actually gave her employer a month's notice...the least she could do for the man who'd stood by her so faithfully for the past three years.

She felt good about her decision, knowing she'd finally made the right one. Her confidence resulted from a very candid talk with J.Q. during which he praised her writing ability and reassured her of her value to the newspaper. He also confirmed Tess's own beliefs that reporting wasn't for everyone and suggested an alternative career possibility she hadn't thought of herself—free-lance writing, which would enable her to work from her home.

He'd even volunteered to prepare her dad for the bombshell, an offer Tess refused. Secure in the knowledge that she finally had her own best interests at heart, Tess believed she could convince her parent of the wisdom of her career change. And thanks to some fatherly advice from J.Q., she also believed her dad would love her in spite of it.

Spirits still up, Tess got out of her vehicle and made her way through the tall pine trees. With every step came vivid memories of the last time she made this walk from car to camper. Her spirits had been up then, too...until Hayden had stepped out of his door.

By the time Tess knocked, her stomach churned with old anxieties and unanswered questions. When Gracie opened the door, Tess took one look at the older woman's face, pale, and her eyes, swollen from crying, and knew, without asking, what she needed to know.

Gracie had talked. And, without a doubt, Gracie now regretted it.

At once, Tess abandoned her plans for a confrontation. The woman had obviously suffered enough. Tess, with her soft heart, could not cause any more pain...even at the expense of a relationship with Hayden.

"Come in," Gracie said.

Without a word, Tess entered the camper. She naturally looked around for Savannah, who was nowhere to be seen.

"Cindy's mother took the kids to breakfast at McDonald's," Gracie said, as though reading her thoughts. She pointed to the couch. "Please have a seat."

"Are you okay?" Tess asked, when they sat side by side on the cushions.

Gracie shook her head.

"Another headache?"

"More like a heartache," Gracie admitted. She sighed, then reached for Tess's hand, which she patted. "I'm glad you're here, my dear. I need to talk to you...to apologize."

Tess tensed, almost dreading to hear the truth verbalized.

"I've done a very foolish thing," Gracie continued. "Something terrible—and well, Hayden blames you for it. I'm going to set him straight as soon as I can, of course, but right now..." Her voice trailed to silence.

"I assume you mean the article on the front page of the *Journal*," Tess reluctantly prompted.

"So you saw it? Yes. I'm the—" she winced "—'source.'" The word came out an emotion-fraught whisper. Gracie's eyes filled with tears, one of which trailed down her colorless cheek. "I don't know how it happened—"

"I do," Tess interjected. "Bo came to your door with some very convincing story—"

"He said he wrote a weekly column on fishing and hunting, and needed recipes for fish and game."

"You invited him in—"

"For that last piece of pie."

"He flattered you—"

"Said I didn't look a day over fifty."

"Began to ask questions about your life on the tournament circuit, your past, Hayden's past and, finally, Sharon's little indiscretion...."

"Exactly!" Gracie exclaimed, clearly astounded. "How on earth did you know?"

"Though I could never trick anyone into talking, myself, I am aware of the technique."

Gracie sighed. "And what a technique. That man could charm the horn off a unicorn."

Silence followed that very astute observation. Then it was Tess's turn to sigh. "I guess Hayden was pretty angry when he saw the story."

Gracie closed her eyes, as though trying to block out a memory. "Angry. Hurt. Sad. I haven't seen him so upset since Sharon ran off that second time. And I guess that's why I didn't confess the truth to him at once...even when I realized he thought you were the one who talked.'' She shook her head. ''I'm so very, very sorry I was such a coward.''

''Forget it,'' Tess told her, giving up for good all plans to ''fight.'' The price of a win was just too high. ''I have.''

''I'll never forget it,'' Gracie said. ''Or what I've done to my nephew. I owe him so much. He paid off my husband's medical bills when he died. Why, if it weren't for Hayden, I'd be out on the street.''

''And if it weren't for you, he'd be struggling to raise his daughter alone. Hayden is very grateful to you for your help.''

Gracie waved away her words. ''Grateful? Yes, but that's not what he'll be when I tell him the truth tonight.''

''So don't tell him,'' Tess said.

Gracie's jaw dropped. ''But I have to.''

''Why?''

''Because it's not fair for him to think you talked.''

''Why?''

''Because you didn't.''

''So what? I'm just a nobody he'll never see again after Sunday,'' Tess said, getting to her feet to pace the room. ''You're his family. Better he should hate me than you.''

''But you're not just a nobody,'' Gracie argued. ''And he doesn't hate you at all. He loves you.''

''Did he say that?'' Tess asked, halting her march to whirl and face Gracie.

''No...''

Tess threw out her hands, palm upward, as good as saying, "so there," even though she didn't utter a word.

"But he didn't have to," Gracie continued, ignoring her dramatics. "I've lived with that man for over two years. I've never seen him happier than this week, beginning the day he met you. It was love at first sight for him, my dear."

"If he loved me, he'd never have assumed I talked," Tess said, sitting down again.

"That was just his subconscious, looking for any excuse to deny his feelings. The man has every reason to resist love, you know."

Tess shrugged, wanting to be, but not quite convinced.

"And as for his hating *me*—" Gracie laughed softly. "You misunderstand my anxiety. I'm not worried about his hating me. Hayden couldn't hate anyone. He will be very disappointed, however, and that's what I can't bear."

"So do as I suggested and keep your secret," Tess said. "It'll be safe with me."

Gracie arched an eyebrow. "What's this? *Your* subconscious looking for any excuse not to love?"

Startled into silence by what might be a very perceptive judgment, Tess had no reply. At once they became aware of a strong wind moaning outside the camper. That eerie sound, coupled with a sudden knock, made both women jump.

Gracie, recovering first, got to her feet and threw open the door, which promptly slammed back against the force of the wind. In rushed Savannah, Cindy and Carla, bringing with them the cool and wet of the storm.

"Have you heard?" Carla exclaimed quite breathlessly.

"Heard what?" Tess and Gracie chorused, exchanging an anxious glance.

"The waves have capsized one of the boats. No one knows which one."

Chapter Ten

Within minutes, Gracie, Tess and Savannah donned all the rain gear they could find and hurried toward the dock, where other worried family members and fishing fans now waited for their fishermen to return to them.

Tess marveled at the intensity of the storm that had descended upon the area so suddenly. Overhead, black clouds churned, raced and dumped torrential rain that a fierce wind swept in sheets across the parking lot and the lake.

Thunder shook the ground every few minutes; lightning danced from cloud to cloud and sometimes forked downward, dangerously near the treetops.

Though Tess knew that only a fool would stand out in such a tempest, she didn't move a muscle to take cover. How could she when the man she loved battled for his life somewhere out on the lake?

And he wasn't alone. Thus far, only four boats of the twenty-five had returned to the safety of the dock, and at the moment, Tess could see only one more headed their way. Mesmerized by fear, she noted how small and helpless that speeding boat looked when it slammed into the massive waves raised by the gale.

The bow of the vessel surged straight upward with every rolling swell and seemed to hang there, while the stern—and the two men aboard—disappeared completely from view behind the waves. Tess's heart hammered like crazy at the sight, and she wondered that the boat didn't flip or sink.

As though preplanned, both Tess and Gracie wound their way through the growing crowd right to the loading area when that lone boat finally docked. Neither stopped until within hearing distance of the fisherman and observer who scrambled out of the rocking craft.

"... Never seen anything like it!" exclaimed one of them, just as a woman, most likely his wife, ran up and engulfed him in a hug of welcome. Tess noted his trembling hands and flushed face. Clearly the race to safety had shaken him as much as it had the woman who waited.

"Neither have I," breathlessly agreed his companion to the tournament personnel and fans now clustered around them. He finger combed his rain-plastered hair, then shook his head. "I'll bet those waves are six-feet high. The boat's full of water. It's a miracle we made it back in one piece."

"Oh, my," Gracie breathed from beside Tess. They exchanged a horror-filled glance.

"Is it true that one of the boats has capsized?" demanded a soaked-to-the-skin, obviously frightened blonde who'd just rushed up.

The fisherman, now standing arm in arm with his wife, hesitated before admitting, "We didn't see one, ma'am, but visibility is terrible...."

He moved off then, headed for cover. Tess didn't blame him a bit, but didn't, for one second, consider doing the same. Instead, she ducked farther back into the hood of the borrowed raincoat she wore and looked out toward the lake again. She discovered that two more boats had appeared on the horizon and were now headed for the dock, bobbing helplessly as kayaks in white-water rapids.

Anxiously, Tess tried to discern the color of the vessels and fought tears of disappointment and new fear when she finally realized that neither was blue, the color of Hayden's.

Over the next hour, this scene repeated itself time and time again. Each and every fisherman who made it to the safety of the shore had a horror story to tell. Tess and Gracie, taking turns holding Savannah, huddled together to stay warm and listened to them all.

The rain poured; the wind moaned; the skies rumbled. Water ran in rivulets down Tess's raincoat and puddled in her tennis shoes. Gracie's umbrella turned inside out; Savannah began to sneeze.

"We're going to wait in our minivan for the others. Want me to take her with us?" It was Carla, holding Cindy and clinging to her precious husband, who'd finally docked his bass boat just minutes before.

"Oh, would you?" Gracie responded with visible relief, handing the exhausted child over to the man.

The four of them took shelter in the van moments later, but Gracie and Tess remained glued to the spot, worriedly scanning the angry skies and treacherous lake for another boat.

The next hour and a half crept by for the women. One by one the fishermen returned until finally boat number twenty-two appeared on the horizon, and soon after, nudged the shore where Tess and Gracie still stood.

Ten minutes after it, boat number twenty-three did the same.

"Is it true that one of the boats has capsized?" croaked the blonde, now nearly frantic, before the latest arrivals could even disembark. Stress and the weather had long since taken their toll on the voice of the woman, who'd asked this same question of each and every fisherman who'd made it in.

Tess, hovering nearby, waited for the now-familiar denial on which she had come to rely. But this time she didn't hear exactly what she expected.

"I did see a boat in trouble," said the man as he climbed out of his vessel, a reply his waiting companion corroborated with a solemn nod. "We turned back to help, but someone else got there before we did and threw them a tow rope." At the woman's stricken expression, he reached out to awkwardly pat her arm. "Now don't you go getting upset. Everyone was okay when I saw them, and I'm going to arrange for some help right now." That said, he smiled, an expression of compassion and reassurance that didn't quite reach his eyes.

Tess narrowed her gaze, noting other telltale signs of anxiety: his clenched fists and the muscle twitching at his temple. Though he put up a good front, she had no doubt this fisherman was as frightened as the rest of them, and her stomach knotted at the realization.

The fisherman and his observer quickly made their way to Carl Trent, president of the ABFA, who stood near the camper that served as tournament office. After a brief but animated conversation, the waterlogged pair went their separate ways. Carl entered the office, only to exit again a couple of minutes later. He scanned the remaining crowd, halting when he spotted Gracie, then elbowed his way over to them.

"Gracie, Janet," he said to Hayden's aunt and the blonde, still standing nearby. "We have a report of trouble." He then repeated what they already knew. "I've called for help from the corps of engineers, and I thought you family members might like to wait inside until we hear something definite."

Family members.

Those words hit Tess like a kick to the back of the knees. She'd never be a family member if Hayden didn't make it back in one piece, and maybe not even then. As far as he was concerned, she had betrayed him—a truth that fear and danger had momentarily shoved right out of her head. Now it returned full force, and with it came regret that they had parted— maybe forever—in such a way.

"I'd rather wait right here," Gracie said to Carl, a sentiment with which Janet quickly agreed.

He nodded his understanding, hugged them both, then walked away to keep a vigil of his own at the water's edge.

Tess tipped her head back, anxiously scanning the skies for some sign of relief from the storm. There was none, however, and blinking against the downpour, she lowered her gaze back to the lake.

"Where are you, Hayden?" she whispered as she studied the horizon.

Fifteen minutes ticked by and then ten more without an appearance by the missing fishermen.

With a heavy sigh, Tess dropped her head forward and slipped a hand inside the hood of the coat to pinch the muscles throbbing at the nape of her neck.

At that moment someone cried out.

Tess jerked to attention at the sound, her eyes back on the turbulent lake. She saw nothing but waves and rain, then...

"Look! Look!" It was Gracie, frantically tugging her sleeve and pointing at what was nothing more than a dark blue in the distance. "There. Do you see? Is it Hayden?"

As one, what crowd that remained tightened up and surged forward, blocking their view. Undaunted, Tess grabbed Gracie's hand and dragged her right to the front, only a few yards from the loading ramp where the boats would dock.

"Is it him?" Gracie repeated, eyes narrowed. "I can't tell...."

"Neither can I." Tess also narrowed her gaze and strained to make out what approached. Gradually the blur in question took on the shape of a boat. That shape then split and separated to become two boats, one of them unmistakably blue and towing the other.

"It's them, Tess! It has to be. Hayden's all right."

With a sob of relief, Tess gave herself up to the older woman's joyous hug. They cried and laughed together, then parted to include Savannah, just running up to join in their celebration.

Gracie, the child now in her arms, hurried right down to the water's edge to meet her nephew, now only yards away. Excited as she was, she didn't notice that Tess hung back, letting the rest of the cheering onlookers slip past until a number of them separated her from the homecoming.

Suddenly certain that Hayden would not be as glad to see her as she was to see him, Tess didn't want to spoil the happy reunion. Maybe later she would get to hold that precious man, she told herself. Maybe after Gracie told him the truth . . . if she ever remembered to do it.

Right now that had to be the last thing on the dear woman's mind, and Tess didn't blame her one bit.

Finally, after what seemed an eternity to Tess, Hayden's boat nudged to a halt against the asphalt ramp. He leapt right out and opened his arms to Gracie and Savannah, both of whom he engulfed in a bear hug.

Impatiently, Tess blinked the moisture—this time tears—from her eyes. She didn't want to miss one marvelous moment of this reunion for which she'd prayed so earnestly these past grueling hours.

Tess noted with satisfaction that the woman named Janet now clung to a lanky young man, no doubt the fisherman who'd had the boat trouble. Nearby, the two observers stood with their families. Well-wishing fans and fellow fishermen surrounded them all. The air filled with excited conversation, hearty congratulations, relieved laughter.

Standing on the outskirts of the joyful confusion, Tess heaved a sigh of relief and closed her eyes to say one last prayer . . . this one of thanks.

"Tess!"

Her eyes flew open at the sound of Hayden's voice, booming over the racket of the crowd. She found him; their gazes locked. To her surprise, he started toward her, a nearly impossible mission in that crush of celebrating humanity.

Heart singing with joy that Gracie had already remembered to set him straight, Tess ran right into the crowd to elbow, push, and even shove her way to her long-lost fisherman. He met her halfway, and wrapping his strong arms around her, lifted her right off the ground in a crushing hug.

"Do you love me, Tess? Do you?" he demanded, much to her surprise.

"I love you," she gasped.

"I love you, too." That said, he pressed his lips to hers in a kiss that left them both breathless. Long moments passed before he raised his head and murmured, "Everything's going to be okay." It took even longer for Tess to reorient to her surroundings enough to realize that Gracie and Savannah had joined them.

"Who's ready to go home?" Hayden asked.

"Me!" his daughter exclaimed, raising her hand and wiggling it like crazy.

Laughing, he stooped to capture that hand and kiss it. Then he scooped Savannah up in his arms and led the way to the camper.

Barely a half hour later found the four of them in dry clothes sitting at the table, Tess and Hayden on one side, Savannah and Gracie on the other. Tess looked down at her borrowed finery—a housecoat of Gracie's—and wrinkled her nose at the sight she must have made.

She sneaked a worried glance at the man she loved so dearly, hoping that her stringy hair and fresh-scrubbed face would not give him second thoughts. Tess found Hayden watching her, a smile of supreme satisfaction on his face and a possessive, rather lustful gleam in his eye.

Tess blushed and looked away, only to discover that Gracie and Savannah, too, stared at her. In the child's eyes she saw open curiosity and conjecture. In Gracie's she saw blatant worry.

Worry? Now that Hayden was safe and sound?

At that moment, Gracie sucked in a deep breath. "Hayden," she blurted. "I have to talk to you about that article you saw in the newspaper last night. The one about Sharon and Wade."

Tess caught her breath. Her eyes grew wide with shock.

Gracie hadn't told him yet? Tess's jaw dropped.

"Why don't we just forget that stupid article?" Hayden said. "What's done is done."

"Yes, and it wasn't done by Tess," Gracie said. "I did it. I'm the one who broke three years of silence, and now everyone knows about Sharon and Wade."

Hayden looked from one to the other of the females watching him so anxiously, then laughed. *Laughed* ... until he realized that Gracie and Tess were about to draw straws to decide who should call the men in white coats.

"I'm sorry," he murmured, clearly struggling for composure. "I'm just so damned relieved it wasn't Tess after all...." He lay an arm across Tess's shoulder and hugged her. "Can you ever forgive me for doubting you?"

"Y-yes," Tess somehow replied. She still hadn't recovered from the timing of Gracie's announcement.

"You mean you're not angry with me?" Gracie demanded, obviously as stunned as Tess if not for the same reason.

"Hell, no."

Gracie digested that for a moment. "But I let you down."

"Nobody's perfect."

"But what about the scandal...?"

"That's Wade's problem," he said.

"But you've worried for years about it," Gracie murmured, exchanging a baffled glance with Tess, who nodded agreement. "And last night you were so angry...."

"Last night and even early this morning," Hayden readily agreed. "And I thought I knew why. But a couple of hours ago, when I was fighting those waves, I finally figured out the real reason I was so upset—not because the truth had been revealed, but because I thought Tess had faked her feelings for me to find it out."

"Is that why you asked me if I loved you?" Tess interjected.

"Yes. I figured that if you did, there was hope for us."

Tess couldn't believe her ears. "You figured that? Even though you believed I'd betrayed your trust?"

He nodded.

"You must be a saint," she commented, awed by his willingness to forgive and forget what he thought she'd done.

"A saint would never have doubted you in the first place, Tess. I'm just a man who understands big dreams and what a novice fisherman—or a budding reporter—might have to do to achieve them."

"But I'm not a budding reporter."

"*What . . . ?*"

"I've turned in my resignation. I leave in one month."

Obviously stunned by her announcement, Hayden stared at her for a full minute without speaking. Then he frowned. "Ah, honey, I hope you didn't do that on my account. I know I've been rather vocal on the subject, but I wouldn't want you to give up the dream of a lifetime."

Tess laughed away his worries. "I did what I did on *my* account . . . for once."

"Have you told your dad?"

"I'm calling him tonight," she replied, at his look of sympathy adding, "It'll be all right. It really will."

Hayden nodded firm agreement with that. "So what are you going to do now?"

"Beats the heck out of me," Tess told him, including everyone in her gaze when she added, "Anyone have any wonderful ideas?"

"I do," Savannah piped up.

"You do? And what's that?" her dad asked.

With a giggle, Savannah beckoned him closer and leaned clear across the table to whisper something in his ear.

Hayden made a great show of considering her words, then shook his head rather thoughtfully. "I don't know, Vanna. That's a pretty tough job."

"What is?" Tess demanded, highly intrigued. "What's the job?"

"You wouldn't be interested," Hayden told her, but his eyes twinkled.

"I think I should be the judge of that," Tess replied. "After you tell me what this position would entail."

He shrugged. "There'd be some cooking."

"I love to cook."

"Yeah? Well, there might be some cleaning, too."

"Go on."

"And an occasional game of Candy Land."

"So far, so good. Tell me more."

"There'd be lots of travel. In fact, you'd be on the road several months out of the year."

"Sounds like fun. What else?"

"You'd have three house mates."

She blinked her surprise. "Did you say... *three?*"

He nodded. "A male and two females, living in very close quarters. So close, in fact, that you'd be expected to sleep with one of them."

"Which one?" she asked, though by now she knew the answer.

"The male," he replied, adding, "But don't worry. He doesn't pull the covers. You might find him on your side of the bed every now and then, though."

"Like on *Nassau Nights,*" Savannah solemnly explained.

Hayden groaned loudly in response to that, while Gracie hid her face in her hands.

Tess bubbled with laughter. "The sleeping arrangements sound very... interesting. So does the job. I do have one question, though. What would I call myself?"

"Stepmother!" Savannah exclaimed, clapping her hands, laughing gleefully at their foolishness. "Isn't my idea wonderful?"

"The best," Tess replied and meant it from the bottom of her heart. "Where do I apply?"

"Right here," Hayden said. "And I can almost guarantee you'll be hired."

"But I don't have experience in this sort of thing and no references, either."

"I'll vouch for your cooking," Gracie said.

"And I'll viche that you play Candy Land," Savannah added, eyes wide with sincerity.

Hayden beamed approval at his family, then gave Tess a big smile. "So what do you say?" he asked. "Are you interested?"

"Only if the position is full time and permanent," Tess replied, looking deep into his eyes.

"Honey, you're one catch this fisherman wouldn't release!"

"Then consider me hooked," she said...and kissed him.

Epilogue

"I can't stand the suspense," Tess moaned. "Is it always like this?"

"I don't know," Gracie responded with a shake of her head. "Hayden's never been so high up in the standings of the Supertourney before."

Tess nodded the truth of that. Stomach knotting, she rested her gaze briefly on Savannah, who snoozed peacefully in her arms. Tess marveled that the child could sleep so soundly amongst such a huge and enthusiastic crowd.

A few yards in front of them, on a tall stage, stood Carl Trent and the next-to-the-last contestant vying for the title "Fisherman of the Year." From the looks of his catch—a limit of large bass—this fisherman had a darned good chance to move from his current position in the standings to first place.

That possibility was corroborated when the weight flashed for all to see. He now led the pack by eighteen pounds and two ounces.

Could Hayden beat that? Tess wondered, stealing a glance offstage at her husband of six whole days. Obviously the tournament officials expected him to do well. Why else would they save his weigh-in until last?

Nonetheless, Tess noted the sweat beading his brow—sweat that could only be the result of nerves since the temperature at Lake Eufala, Oklahoma, the site of the tournament, was unseasonably mild for August.

Poor baby, she thought, at once sympathetic with her precious spouse. For years, he'd dreamed of winning the Supertourney. Would today be the day?

"Why, hello there." Both Tess and Gracie looked toward the source of that greeting, a tall woman who slipped into the empty seat next to Hayden's aunt.

Gracie's face lit up. "Hello, yourself. I haven't seen you in ages." She turned to Tess. "Tess, this is an old friend of mine, Stephanie West. Steph, meet Tess Bogart, Hayden's new wife."

"Hayden's married?" Stephanie gave Tess a great big smile. "Well, it's about time. Congratulations, Tess. You've got yourself a man in a million."

"I think so," Tess agreed.

"That's Stephanie's husband over there," Gracie told Tess, pointing toward a nice-looking man who'd registered his catch earlier.

"I missed seeing his weigh-in," Stephanie said. "This job I have right now is a killer. Seems like I work all the time." She heaved a weary sigh. "Do you work, Tess?"

"I'm a free-lance writer and an instructor at the Wilson Writing Institute," Tess said. "Have you heard of it?"

Stephanie nodded. "Oh, sure. Aren't the classes done by correspondence?"

"Yes," Tess said.

"So you're free to travel the circuit with Hayden?"

"That's right."

Stephanie sighed again, this time rather wistfully. "Lucky lady."

Lucky lady. The comment echoed in Tess's head. She smiled, not for the first time acknowledging the truth of that. Only a "lucky lady" could find so loving a husband and so wonderful a ready-made family. Only a "lucky lady" would have a dad so supportive of her career change that he would buy her a laptop computer as a wedding present.

"And here's our last fisherman, folks, Hayden Bogart," boomed Carl Trent into the microphone. "He's currently in second place."

Tess tensed and sat up straighter in her chair to watch Hayden walk across the stage, clutching the bag of fish that would make or break him this day.

"Now Hayden, here, is one of our most dedicated contestants," Carl said. "So dedicated that he and his brand-new bride spent their honeymoon in a bass boat, practice-fishing the waters of this beautiful lake." The crowd cheered its opinion of that. "Will it pay off for him?" Carl asked them, milking the moment for all it was worth. "Let's see."

He took Hayden's bag and laid it in the weigh basket. Unable to bear the suspense, Tess closed her eyes.

"Twenty pounds, three ounces!" Carl yelled. "We have a winner, folks! We have a winner!"

Instantly the crowd went wild. Savannah woke with a start, clearly frightened and clinging to Tess.

"Your daddy won the tournament, Vanna," Tess said, hugging her close to reassure her. "He won."

"Cross your heart?" Savannah asked, obviously having trouble assimilating the news.

"Cross my heart," Tess said even as Carl instructed Hayden to bring his family up on stage. Since a laughing Gracie refused to budge from her seat, Tess and Savannah had to go alone. Seconds later, they joined Hayden on the platform, where he engulfed them both in a hug of victory.

"So what are you going to buy with all the money?" Carl teased Tess after Hayden finally released her and took Savannah.

"A second honeymoon," Tess replied without hesitation.

"And where do you want to spend *this* one?" Carl asked.

"Indoors," Tess said, a reply that earned her a big grin from her husband and a roar of approval from the crowd.

*   *   *   *   *

HE'S MORE THAN A MAN, HE'S ONE OF OUR

EMMETT
Diana Palmer

What a way to start the new year! Not only is Diana Palmer's EMMETT the first of our new series, FABULOUS FATHERS, but it's her 10th LONG, TALL TEXANS and her 50th book for Silhouette!

Emmett Deverell was at the end of his lasso. His three children had become uncontrollable! The long, tall Texan knew they needed a mother's influence, and the only female offering was Melody Cartman. Emmett would rather be tied to a cactus than deal with that prickly woman. But Melody proved to be softer than he'd ever imagined....

Don't miss Diana Palmer's EMMETT, available in January.

Fall in love with our FABULOUS FATHERS—and join the Silhouette Romance family!

ROMANCE™

FF193

NORA ROBERTS

Love has a language all its own, and for centuries flowers have symbolized love's finest expression. Discover the language of flowers—and love—in this romantic collection of 48 favorite books by bestselling author Nora Roberts.

Two titles are available each month at your favorite retail outlet.

In December, look for:

Partners, Volume #21
Sullivan's Woman, Volume #22

In January, look for:

Summer Desserts, Volume #23
This Magic Moment, Volume #24

Collect all 48 titles
and become fluent in

THE LANGUAGE of LOVE

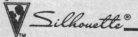

Silhouette®

LOL1292

OFFICIAL RULES • MILLION DOLLAR MATCH 3 SWEEPSTAKES
NO PURCHASE OR OBLIGATION NECESSARY TO ENTER

To enter, follow the directions published. **ALTERNATE MEANS OF ENTRY:** Hand print your name and address on a 3″×5″ card and mail to either: Silhouette "Match 3," 3010 Walden Ave., P.O. Box 1867, Buffalo, NY 14269-1867, or Silhouette "Match 3," P.O. Box 609, Fort Erie, Ontario L2A 5X3, and we will assign your Sweepstakes numbers. (Limit: one entry per envelope.) For eligibility, entries must be received no later than March 31, 1994. No responsibility is assumed for lost, late or misdirected entries.

Upon receipt of entry, Sweepstakes numbers will be assigned. To determine winners, Sweepstakes numbers will be compared against a list of randomly preselected prizewinning numbers. In the event all prizes are not claimed via the return of prizewinning numbers, random drawings will be held from among all other entries received to award unclaimed prizes.

Prizewinners will be determined no later than May 30, 1994. Selection of winning numbers and random drawings are under the supervision of D.L. Blair, Inc., an independent judging organization, whose decisions are final. One prize to a family or organization. No substitution will be made for any prize, except as offered. Taxes and duties on all prizes are the sole responsibility of winners. Winners will be notified by mail. Chances of winning are determined by the number of entries distributed and received.

Sweepstakes open to persons 18 years of age or older, except employees and immediate family members of Torstar Corporation, D.L. Blair, Inc., their affiliates, subsidiaries and all other agencies, entities and persons connected with the use, marketing or conduct of this Sweepstakes. All applicable laws and regulations apply. Sweepstakes offer void wherever prohibited by law. Any litigation within the province of Quebec respecting the conduct and awarding of a prize in this Sweepstakes must be submitted to the Régies des Loteries et Courses du Quebec. In order to win a prize, residents of Canada will be required to correctly answer a time-limited arithmetical skill-testing question. Values of all prizes are in U.S. currency.

Winners of major prizes will be obligated to sign and return an affidavit of eligibility and release of liability within 30 days of notification. In the event of non-compliance within this time period, prize may be awarded to an alternate winner. Any prize or prize notification returned as undeliverable will result in the awarding of that prize to an alternate winner. By acceptance of their prize, winners consent to use of their names, photographs or other likenesses for purposes of advertising, trade and promotion on behalf of Torstar Corporation without further compensation, unless prohibited by law.

This Sweepstakes is presented by Torstar Corporation, its subsidiaries and affiliates in conjunction with book, merchandise and/or product offerings. Prizes are as follows: Grand Prize—$1,000,000 (payable at $33,333.33 a year for 30 years). First through Sixth Prizes may be presented in different creative executions, each with the following approximate values: First Prize—$35,000; Second Prize—$10,000; 2 Third Prizes—$5,000 each; 5 Fourth Prizes—$1,000 each; 10 Fifth Prizes—$250 each; 1,000 Sixth Prizes—$100 each. Prizewinners will have the opportunity of selecting any prize offered for that level. A travel-prize option, if offered and selected by winner, must be completed within 12 months of selection and is subject to hotel and flight accommodations availability. Torstar Corporation may present this Sweepstakes utilizing names other than Million Dollar Sweepstakes. For a current list of all prize options offered within prize levels and all names the Sweepstakes may utilize, send a self-addressed, stamped envelope (WA residents need not affix return postage) to: Million Dollar Sweepstakes Prize Options/Names, P.O. Box 4710, Blair,[fj NE 68009.

The Extra Bonus Prize will be awarded in a random drawing to be conducted no later than May 30, 1994 from among all entries received. To qualify, entries must be received by March 31, 1994 and comply with published directions. No purchase necessary. For complete rules, send a self-addressed, stamped envelope (WA residents need not affix return postage) to: Extra Bonus Prize Rules, P.O. Box 4600, Blair, NE 68009.

For a list of prizewinners (available after July 31, 1994) send a separate, stamped, self-addressed envelope to: Million Dollar Sweepstakes Winners, P.O. Box 4728, Blair, NE 68009.   SWP-1292

VOWS
A series celebrating marriage
by Sherryl Woods

To Love, Honor and Cherish—these were the words that three
generations of Halloran men promised their women they'd live
by. But these vows made in love are each challenged by the
tests of time....

In October—Jason Halloran meets his match in *Love* #769;
In November—Kevin Halloran rediscovers love—with his
wife—in *Honor* #775;
In December—Brandon Halloran rekindles an old flame in
Cherish #781.

These three stirring tales are coming down the aisle toward
you—only from Silhouette Special Edition!

Silhouette Christmas Stories 1992

Experience the beauty of Yuletide romance with Silhouette Christmas Stories 1992—a collection of heartwarming stories by favorite Silhouette authors.

JONI'S MAGIC by Mary Lynn Baxter
HEARTS OF HOPE by Sondra Stanford
THE NIGHT SANTA CLAUS RETURNED by Marie Ferrarrella
BASKET OF LOVE by Jeanne Stephens

Also available this year are three popular early editions of Silhouette Christmas Stories—1986, 1987 and 1988. Look for these and you'll be well on your way to a complete collection of the best in holiday romance.

Plus, as an added bonus, you can receive a FREE keepsake Christmas ornament. Just collect four proofs of purchase from any November or December 1992 Harlequin or Silhouette series novels, or from any Harlequin or Silhouette Christmas collection, and receive a beautiful dated brass Christmas candle ornament.

Mail this certificate along with four (4) proof-of-purchase coupons, plus $1.50 postage and handling (check or money order—do not send cash), payable to Silhouette Books, to: **In the U.S.:** P.O. Box 9057, Buffalo, NY 14269-9057; **In Canada:** P.O. Box 622, Fort Erie, Ontario, L2A 5X3.

ONE PROOF OF PURCHASE

Name: _____
_____
Address: _____
_____
City: _____
State/Province: _____
Zip/Postal Code: _____

SX92POP

093 KAG